ENTRY LEVEL

ENTRY LEVEL

stories

WENDY WIMMER

AUTUMN
HOUSE PRESS

Autumn House Press receives state arts funding support through a grant from the Pennsylvania Council on the Arts, a state agency funded by the Commonwealth of Pennsylvania.

This project is supported in part by the National Endowment for the Arts. To find out more about how National Endowment for the Arts grants impact individuals and communities, visit www.arts.gov.

ISBN: 9781637680582
Library of Congress Control Number: 2022940891

Book & cover design by Joel W. Coggins

FOR SHIRLEY SUELFLOHN HOUSE

MY GRANDMOTHER, WHO TOLD THE VERY BEST STORIES

CONTENTS

Strange Magic   **3**

Ghosting   **14**

Where She Went   **33**

Fuse   **45**

Lower Midnight   **51**

INGOB   **55**

Passeridae   **71**

Texts from Beyond   **86**

Flarby   **95**

Seven Minutes in Heaven   **108**

Car People   **115**

Intersomnolence   **129**

Billet-Doux   **145**

Feðgin   **162**

The Bog King   **165**

Acknowledgments   **177**

Thank Yous   **179**

ENTRY LEVEL

STRANGE MAGIC

WHEN MARY ELLEN'S LEFT BREAST GREW BACK ON ITS OWN DURING OUR Saturday dinner break, we had confirmation that something weird was happening.

It was between shifts at the Rola-Rena: a private Cub Scout party had just left and our Saturday Night Late Skate didn't open for another two hours. "Wasted Skate" was our little staff secret—two hours to kill and a twenty-four pack of Old Milwaukee because these days we weren't likely to party after closing down and were more likely to collapse a lung trying to hurdle the mop bucket like we used to twenty years back.

Mary Ellen's mastectomy scar had been hurting like crazy all night, she'd said. I'd spied her from the DJ booth, touching the pack of Virginia Slims she carried in a jeweled leather pouch in her breast pocket as though the stiff cardboard were poking her scar. She had limped off the rink slowly, her whole left arm collapsed against her side. We were all pretty used to Mary Ellen disappearing from time to time, between the smoke breaks and her chemo panics, you just trusted she'd pop back up before you missed her.

Vera had gone into the restroom to pee and caught Mary Ellen with her blouse open, not even in a stall. Mary Ellen was inspecting the scar where her nipple used to be. The angry red puckered monster was scabbed and weeping, even though it had been healed over for seven months. She told Vera that she figured there was nothing to do until the late skate was done, so she popped an Advil, and then I happened to play a particularly lovely ELO flashback mega mix, which coaxed her back onto the rink. During the swell of the Moog organ, Mary Ellen took a nasty spill in the back turn. She was usually a ballerina on her Riedell Quads, so my first thought was that one of those little Cub Scout cocksuckers had dropped a lollipop stick on the rink. I skated over to help her up, and she reached into her blouse and pulled out her falsie, then felt up her reemerged cancer-riddled titty.

Nothing made sense, but when you're staring at a breast that defies all reasoning, you start adding up all the facts real quick. We all started comparing notes. It wasn't just Mary Ellen's prodigal breast. Vera pointed out that she was somehow gaining three pounds per shift, even though she'd cut back to 672 calories a day, a precise number because it consisted of three Kessler and Diet Cokes plus two dry pieces of toasted diet bread. Each of us had held onto the observation that our fingernails weren't growing as fast as they used to, weren't growing at all, actually. We'd all hoarded that secret shame, assuming our worst fears were finally coming home to roost: After all the years of drinking and pharmaceutical recreation, our bodies must have finally called a time-out. But, it turns out, after twenty years of taking care of the rink, that old rink had decided to return the favor.

Randy thought we were all full of shit, but then after five laps to Michael Jackson's "Thriller," he felt the memory of his bruised shin return like he'd only just slammed the car door shut on it that second. The skin was a mean purple, but after two more laps, the pain and the bruise were both gone. Then he fell to the ground, skates splayed out in front of him, bent his head, and said Hail Marys until "Year of the Cat" ended.

"Time Passages" by Al Stewart seemed to have the best effect, although anything by Fogelberg or The Alan Parsons Project worked good too. The Bee Gees worked a little too well, if you know what I mean, made our eyes feel swimmy, like our brains were remapping the colors and state capitals.

It might have been the disco ball, hanging since the Rola-Rena opened in 1972. Or it might have been the skates, an aggregation of forty-odd years of foot sweat and popped blisters reaching critical mass, leaking back up through our soles. Or it might just have been the new formula of the blue raspberry slushie that we were testing out, a blend of high-fructose corn syrup, energy drink, and enough fake flavor and coloring to make it glow under the black lights.

Kyle made us stop every five minutes and measured the length of our hair and fingernails and asked us a few questions that had no rhyme or reason. Did we need to go to the bathroom? Did we feel tingling in our extremities? What day was it? What year was it? What was three times four? How did you spell "shish kebab"? Randy didn't know how to spell it, but the fact that he consistently misspelled it was good enough for Kyle.

After an hour, Kyle had amassed some data to form a few hypotheses: Counterclockwise worked; clockwise didn't. The disco ball needed to be spinning, but the data was inconclusive on whether the laser beams had any effect. There were some issues with more modern music, leaving us feeling older and anguished in a deep way, like after you've been crying a long time. But heavy synths from the early '80s seemed to have the best return on our time investment. The rink was erasing anywhere between a day to a week every time you circled. Your body was getting younger, going back through time, anywhere from a week to a month in the spread of five minutes.

As soon as we put a calculation to it, we all shut up and started skating really fast.

My calves felt itchy, unused, a sense of growth in my spine; I felt taller. Somewhere in the last decade, I had gotten an inch shorter. My doc had said it was spine compression because of all the vitamins that were leaching out of my blood stream. He told me my bones belonged to a man twice my age.

We all should have been winded from skating miles around the rink, but each lap felt like a new start, as though it erased the one before it. Running around the rink without skates on didn't seem to do anything. Kyle had a theory about spatial contact and rogue sound waves that no one cared to listen to. I needed to do more laps. We all needed to. Time could have been running out for all we knew.

"We should close the rink."

"We can't tell anyone else about this," I said, pointedly staring at Randy, who concentrated on tightening and retightening his laces. Randy was on probation and could get sent back to jail for even being near all these kids. We made sure he was never alone with any of them, but that wouldn't matter to his probation officer. If we told and the news got out, Randy would be right back in jail.

"What are we going to tell the owner?" Vera's buttons were

straining. I hadn't noticed it, but she'd been slowly losing weight over the last few years. Still, she looked healthier, having rolled back something like six months or more at that point.

"Asbestos removal," Kyle said, squinting. He was twentysome-thing, but already the boy had soft, supple middle-aged hips that reminded me of slow dancing. He held a pair of skates by the laces, the way you might hold a dead rat.

"Them kids," Vera said, fiddling with her heart monitor wrist-watch. "What's it going to do to them? How many times does a kid skate around a rink? Twenty? Thirty?"

The implications were tough—losing twenty or thirty days was nothing for used-up bodies like ours. But kids, that was a different story. The potty training gone to hell, the forgotten ability to tie their own shoes or speak. We all looked around and nodded, half thinking about the children and not wanting to admit that we were also thinking about having more time on the rink. Or less time, if you think about it that way.

Vera was flipping through the events calendar and announced, "Derby."

The derby team practiced at the Rena every Saturday and Tues-day and could really rack up the rotations. A lot of strong skaters who couldn't even get on the team unless they could circle the rink twenty-five times in five minutes. They'd un-age a full year in a sin-gle practice. They'd use up the rink's youth juice, and they didn't need it. Not like us.

Vera made us all do pinky swears for the lack of a suitable bible. "For now," we said, as though we'd make any other decision until the miracle of the rink stopped working. We made a sign on the clean side of a Dr Pepper box:

ASBESTOS! TBA

Normally, you don't think about how many times you do laps. If you do, you start to get a little dizzy, go all Camus about the futility of the situation. Your laces on the right side start to get loose from always turning against them. Normally I switch it up, do a little fancy footwork and skate backward for a bit, but what if that messed up the youth magic? What if I sped up time instead of reversing it and my face melted off like the Nazis when they opened the Ark of the Covenant?

We had been so excited about the discovery that we didn't notice that Mary Ellen still hadn't come back from the bathroom after her breast reunited with its beautiful partner. I could see her through the little window in the DJ booth, whenever I'd go in to change the songs. She was standing out back behind the dumpster in her stocking feet, taking long drags off her cigarette, occasionally touching her left breast, feeling for the area where there had been a lump. Or there was a lump again. She had a slushie cup that she was using as an ashtray, the butts collecting in blue raspberry melt. I threw on the soundtrack to *Xanadu*. I could hear Kyle asking Randy if he thought the rink could be used for other means, philosophical questions. "Just bring a special lady here for a friendly skate. If she were knocked up, not that you'd know or even be sure, but that thing would just be gone. She wouldn't even feel it. She wouldn't even need to know what was happening. Just skated out of reality, are you feeling me? And then a guy would be off the hook, and it wouldn't be a sin. This is God's way—this is an act of God; you get what I'm saying?"

Randy was muttering, making negative sounds.

I rubbed my bicep. The skin didn't feel as rubbery. When had it gotten rubbery? I hadn't noticed, sometime over the last five years, apparently. Mary Ellen needed to get in on this, more than any of us. I leaned my head out the back door, feeling the rise of Olivia Newton-John's sweet vocals pulling me to skate.

"You coming in and knocking down some laps?" I was careful to not let my skates hit the pavement, my front wheels locked over the doorjamb. The owner was insane about the chastity of the skate floor: We swore she could spot street grit with a sixth sense, but I also didn't want to impact the sanctity of the connection between the skates and the unending oval time rift that we were freestyling on.

"Diet Coke tasted like dirt or needles for so long after the chemo. It just started tasting right a few weeks ago." Her hand went to touch her left breast but then stopped in midair.

"The tum— the lump is back?" It was a punch in the gut, the idea that roller skating had regrown tissue. Everything it was taking from us, it had given something back too.

The question loitered between us in the alley. If you didn't know better, you'd never believe she was the girl in the oxidized photos from the '80s that still hung in the rink locker room. Somewhere along the way, her forehead had cast a long divot between her eyebrows and a constellation of pockmarks on her chin and cheeks from God only knows what. A feather of a scar curved down from the corner of her lip, so soft and light it seemed that it was a missed stripe of lipstick. Mary Ellen had taken a headfirst dive off a boyfriend's Harley about a decade back. She probably should have gotten stitches, but the boyfriend had been drinking and doing a little pharmaceutical, so they didn't dare go to the ER. Then he dumped her a month later, saying that he lost his boner when he looked at her ruined face.

And now I'd get to see the lady unspool, undo the decline of the early 2000s and the pessimism of the '90s. Roll back through the hip-hop years, slide past grunge, and then coast through synth pop, all the way back to looking fine in her Levi's. I'd only been nine or ten when I first started coming to the rink, but Mary Ellen's clipped business voice as she dished out your skates, followed by her amazing sideways and trick footwork during the slow periods had made me curse our age difference even then. I had vowed to marry her someday. Of course, somehow, we never managed. Back then, I'd practiced my tricks and jumps, but then came the war and the sand, and I put the rink behind me. When I was working my way off the needle, during the worst of the anhedonia, I'd get a beautiful vision of her swishing through the brain fog—a blur of tight satin pants and lip gloss. Had to look her up once I made it past the night sweats and found she was still at the rink. So I ended up with a job that was meant to last me for a little while. That was over a decade ago. Sometimes it's too easy being easy.

A shout erupted from the rink, over the sweet, mellow licks of O.N.J.'s vocal Xanax. I skated back over the carpet and into the rink, to the center where Kyle was curled into a fetal position, as though he'd been gut punched. Randy and Vera hovered over him nervously.

Kyle struggled to his knees and dry heaved, letting one string of spit slowly drip toward the floor. He had the grace to catch it with his hand and wipe it on his pants. He motioned for a pull up, and we all stood in an awkward silence, looking at Randy, who was the lowest on our pecking order, the one who knew that he'd be kicked out if he made himself even a tiny pain in the ass. Randy obliged and stuck his hands in the front pockets of his jeans for a discrete wipe.

Kyle looked shiny and undercooked, like raw chicken beneath cellophane. His eyebrows were completely gone, and his hair was all short and bristly. "Don't skate too close to the epicenter," Kyle finally said. "It really fucking sucks."

He limped back to the side, picked up his reporter's notebook, and panting, fell onto the nearest bench. I was impressed that he knew the word "epicenter." Above us, the disco ball was an unblinking eye.

"Dancing Queen" queued automatically, as though the ancient MP3 shuffler was making an editorial comment, urging us to continue to *circle circle circle*. Vera squealed in approval and shoved off, hugging the wall. Her pale doughy stomach peeped out where her shirt had popped a button. Judging by the size of her ass, she had to be coasting back into the winter months of three years ago, when she'd been her heaviest. She skated with a need to feel her jeans get looser, to know that she was skating closer and closer to some version of herself that loved her thighs. Mary Ellen had come back in and was carrying her skates back over to the bench. I watched her for a minute to see if she was going to put them back on, but it seemed like she wasn't sure either.

"Hey."

"Hey." Her face had gone slack and sallow, her eyes bright. A few times, Randy had mentioned that he thought Mary Ellen was tweaked. She had never seemed that way to me. Now a sweetness clung to her, like burnt cinnamon and old hair spray. We always thought the crack pipes in the back alley were from the hobos that liked to dig through the rink's garbage for half-eaten Super Ropes. Maybe they weren't.

Randy skated past us and shouted, "Woo!" as "Like a Virgin" automatically played. It was Randy's theme song. He got a little too excited about music with heavy innuendo, songs that usually made the rest of us uncomfortable, but in my quest for early '80s music,

I had forgotten to remove it from the playlist. Maybe we were all involved in some kind of collective acid trip. Maybe there was a mold in the rink, the kind that made the girls in Salem all go crazy and then get tried as witches. Had they thought they were getting younger? Had they imagined that body parts were growing back on their own?

"Eben!" Vera shouted across the rink to me. "No Madonna! Madonna doesn't work!"

She had ditched her blouse and was now wearing just her bra, her body glistening with sweat. Randy was taking in the view, weaving behind her like a mako shark behind a seal. Kyle's entire skull seemed to glow under the skin. I pushed off the wall with enough force to ruffle the Coke advertisements stuck to the side. *Lava! Hot lava!* A child's voice played in my head. Going back a day at a time seemed a safe rate. Best not to screw with the natural order too much. Dabbling, that was what we were doing. Dabbling. Nothing serious. Nothing like Mary Ellen's consequences.

What you forget to think about is the logistics of the situation. You couldn't think about it because you wanted it too badly. Instead, you think about the hairline you had when you were seventeen. You think about the way you could stroke off forty times a day and only so few because you had to sleep and go to school during the rest of the time. You think about how each of your coworkers are skating back days they already spent inside this former fallout shelter, spinning hot dogs on heated spindles and handing out Skee-Ball tickets to eight-year-olds. You think about how you could do things over, how if you could go back again you could ask Mary Ellen for a date.

And then she wouldn't ever have had to date criminals and assholes and take up smoking and get cancer and a ruined face and a mouth that over time had formed a perpetual frown, like tire ruts in a gravel driveway. Enough time and you could go to college with the incoming freshmen, get a real degree and not some late-night television infomercial certificate of technology that meant nothing when you actually tried to get a job somewhere that needed a résumé instead of a paper application.

Mary Ellen had her purse on her shoulder and was clipping her lighter to her jeweled leather cigarette pouch, the conclusive movement that signaled the end of every shift since I'd known her.

"You're not going to skate anymore?" I shouted over The Hollies' "The Air That I Breathe."

She shook her head and pressed her lips together. A delicate asterisk of lipstick wept into the creases of her lips when she did that, years of pursing to inhale on her smokes. She bumped the door open with her butt and for a moment, she was cast in shadow, backlit by the golden cast of an orange sunset. She paused again, and I skated over the carpet, reaching to steady myself at the cashier's table. The front wheel of my skate kissed the entryway, but she was already walking backward into the parking lot.

GHOSTING

THE INSURANCE COMPANY SENT OVER A FAT NURSE. THERE WAS NO POLITE way to put it—she was fat. No matter what would happen, no matter what I said, no matter that she was only there to make sure my mother remembered to flush the toilet and didn't set herself on fire, Marlene was fat.

And I was fatter.

I admit, I had let myself go. Not that I went to the gym much before Evelyn's illness, but now I spent every night making her dinner, and later, while she was glued to CNN in the den, I was consulting Dr. Google, trying to Sherlock my way through the litany of human ailments and puzzle out Evelyn's unspecific mental deterioration. If a genie could have granted me three wishes, up until my mother began to lose her mind, my first wish would have been the ability to eat whatever I wanted without anyone knowing and without getting fat. Now, I would be happy with an answer, a specific culprit to blame for her acute dementia. Okay, Wish Number Two would still involve me breaking into KFC under the cover of darkness and eating the Original Recipe-coated skin off dozens of chickens.

Evelyn's living and breathing doctor had tentatively diagnosed her with acute dementia but was at a loss for a root cause of why her mind was now filled with word salad. That was the official term—word salad—like the contents of a library secretary's lunch. Most doctors golfed; Evelyn's was a hunter. During our first meeting, I stared at pictures of him holding limp ducks, lolling stag heads, straddling a bear pornographically. There hadn't been a stroke, and Evelyn was too young for Alzheimer's, so he sighed and said that we were now shooting at her condition with scattershot. He handed me a pamphlet about aging and senility, even though Evelyn was only in her early fifties. They give you a pamphlet when your mother loses her mind. The pamphlet does not tell you where to find it.

Today, there were six very expensive prescription bottles in my purse, six bottles that were so expensive that I had had to put them on my credit card. Four were for Evelyn—two mood enhancers, a sleeping remedy, and a neuro-stimulant that had been very successful in staving off the kind of unspecified dementia my mother was experiencing.

Thanks to Marlene and her acrylic pants with the pilled fabric from where her thighs rubbed against themselves, the other prescriptions were for me. One was a new weight loss drug that stopped calories from being absorbed by the body. The fat itself would be skimmed off my food chemically, sucked into some kind of bowel sponge, and shat back into the toilet. The other was a special vitamin to replace the fat-soluble vitamins that were also blocked. The hunter/doctor had fixed my weight in his sights on the chart, circled it, and trailed over his letters twice, engraving the paper with his blue BIC pen.

After the doctor's office, I had gone to McDonald's and gotten a Combo Meal #1: Big Mac, french fries, and a Diet Coke. Yes, the irony was clear, but the diet drug didn't do anything about the sugar part of the calorie equation, so Diet Coke it was. I drove to a park and ate in the car, half-expecting a rap on the window from a concerned passerby. It was the greatest trick ever concocted! Fattening food, no consequences! The audacity. The inevitable conclusion to lunch was an orange slick that solidified as it clung to the cold porcelain of the toilet in the office and stubbornly remained after flushing, a type of fecal stigmata, or perhaps a halo of virtuous poop. I ate that? Fascinating. The products of my daily consumption sorted tidily into That Which Is Good and That Which Is Not. You almost had to admire the efficiency, like some kind of mechanical process. I never understood Freud's theory of evolving from the lascivious oral latency stage into the anal period, but now I got it—the very act of expelling one's shit was extraordinary. A strange hit of sadness washed over me as I flushed, wondering which exact pound it was that I was flushing? One of the Freshman Fifteen? The pint of Ben and Jerry's that was the death of my favorite pair of jeans when I was twenty-four? Or maybe something more recent, like the bag of Funyuns I inhaled while packing up my apartment two months ago? Goodbye little bit of Fat Grace! We barely knew ye.

*　　*　　*

"Men don't listen to ugly women," Evelyn had liked to say, which is why Gloria Steinem made such a stir in the press. She'd point out Gloria's nipples visible through her white T-shirt, and she was positive that Gloria's pretty Playboy Bunny eyes had more than just a little to do with the feminist movement. The irony of this criticism was not lost on anyone in our household, for me or any of Evelyn's rotating live-in boyfriends who aligned with and furthered any variety of liberal pursuits. Larry the yogi, Clive the British curator, Sam the alderman and eventual failed mayoral candidate, I had lost track of them all. Evelyn thought of her bed like a trapdoor spider, capturing the interest and monetary resources of her romantic partners, although not as simple as quid pro quo. The men always just wanted to *do things* for her, it wasn't her fault, she'd sniff. Evelyn's own lovely figure was always for a cause, any cause, whichever cause it was that week. She had shed her flower child past like a pair of soiled underwear, taking to the picket sign and bullhorn like they were extensions of her own pale Southern belle arm. Men still held doors open for her. "It can't be helped," she'd say, "and it's just common courtesy anyway."

I, on the other hand, had begun to swell shortly after leaving the efficient, sparse quarters of Evelyn's womb. I grew out of my "Wanted Baby" T-shirts quickly and was wearing a "Wanted Child" T-shirt much faster than my playmates, other children with names like Sunny and Giacamo. My birth certificate says I am "Jehovah's Holy Grace," born shortly after Evelyn spent her summer in Israel, shouting "Menstruation is natural and clean" to the Orthodox men walking to the synagogue. Evelyn started calling me Grace by the time I was three. What a relief—only racehorses have a possessive noun for a first name.

Someone once called me "reasonably attractive," which I understood was shorthand for "You're not absolutely ugly, but I don't want to sleep with you at this juncture." I knew I wasn't going to be walking the runway as a model or collecting dollars in my G-string, dancing on a bar. I got knowledge jobs in spite of my fat ass. And that never really mattered to me. Work came first. Single and vibrantly exciting opportunities! These are the things single women tell themselves. All of those things Evelyn espoused from behind her clipboard, her shiny Vidal Sassoon bob and noisy wooden platform heels drawing attention as she picketed for unions, for childcare, for the freedom for women to have and do and be all things. And her love life was part of her alluring package. It never hurt her causes if she happened to date a few corporate lawyers or oil execs in the name of progress. "You're smart, Grace," she'd say back then. "You are destined for greatness."

However, that was before I was fatter than Marlene.

*   *   *

Walking into Evelyn's house, I nodded to Marlene and lined the six new pill bottles on the counter with the rest. It was like a natural history museum display, primitive bugs that moved too slow and got trapped in tree resin. Marlene grabbed her purse and headed out the door.

What did Marlene's house look like? How would she react if I just showed up one day, dug through her snack cupboard, and then collapsed onto her sofa, letting my car drip oil on her driveway?

"Mooooauh!" Evelyn interrupted my fantasy with a quick burst of wordless surprise.

Has she hurt herself? Burned? No, more likely a paper cut or another ghost of a dead relative. Evelyn was standing in front of the television screen, her hand pressed against her flat stomach.

"The baby! I felt it kick! Oh great. I must be further along than they think." Her hand was trembling over the elastic waistband of her khakis.

"Evelyn, you're not having a baby."

"I'm having a baby. Ask the doctor." I thought for a moment about calling her doctor and posing this question, just to see what kind of metaphor he'd use for her uterus. Good money on the one about the dog that won't hunt.

Ah! Evelyn had been looking at a parenting magazine at the doctor's office. She had been interested in the faces of babies recently, although I wasn't sure where that was coming from. Evelyn didn't like babies. She had always insisted I call her Evelyn, stating simply that the mewling throngs of other women's children screeching "Mommy" gave her a headache. Starting at age six, however, I had rebelled and started calling her "Mother," stressing the second syllable until it became its own word. Even now, in my brain, I sometimes think of Evelyn as Muth Err first and have to remind myself to call her Evelyn.

I placed my hand on her tight stomach, wondering if it was a tumor or something. Maybe it was a bowel blockage? A hernia? Goodness knows, Evelyn might have hurt herself the other day when she decided to start moving around the furniture in her bedroom. I had secretly hoped that she would decide she hated that pillow-topped Sealy and would want to trade me for the futon I'd been sleeping on in the study. The futon was a remnant from another live-in, Larry, who had smelled of essential oils. In fact, at night, I could still smell the sandalwood, and the thought of sleeping in Larry's chakras made me itch all over. He had tried to teach me yoga, put me in downward dog and then told me to actualize my sphincter. Then demonstrated. Larry was kicked to the curb, minus one futon and several greasy foam mats that reminded me of giant, used flip-flops.

"Hmm." Under my hand, Evelyn's stomach made a definite gurgle. What to do? Call the doctor back? Then I heard the telltale muffled rumble of an intestinal shift. I turned her by the shoulders and pointed her at the bathroom. "You're about to give birth any minute."

"Gracie, I don't care for your tone."

Her slippers padded across the hardwood. This was the hall-mark of all quiet finales: the scuffing of rubber soles across hallways and the smell of Vicks VapoRub. When she returned, I went in to flush the toilet for her while she settled into her favored spot on the sofa, seemingly back to normal, blanching when the president's face popped on the screen.

"Fucking fucks."

Evelyn never swore before the dementia. She felt it showed intellectual weakness. Now on the new medication, she punctuat-ed our evenings with shits and fucks and piss, hard Anglo-Saxon consonants that I admit were strangely satisfying. I suspected this newfound swearing was due to Marlene's taste in daytime televi-sion shows, so I only allowed thirty minutes of CNN in the evening. Evelyn enjoyed nothing more than her vehemence for government. "Look at those pissants!" she'd cry. "They aren't so much now, those fucks." She would lean toward the glowing screen like a baseball pitcher about to throw a strike. Her expression was exactly the same as when she stood behind podiums and encouraged women to take back the night. It was fascinating. She didn't like it when I watched her, so I often hid behind a floor lamp, nibbling a piece of pillowy, soft white bread spread with peanut butter until she'd no-tice me and shoo me like she was flapping away a bee.

*　　*　　*

A month later, there was no change in Evelyn, but I knew that my own pills were working when Marlene checked me out one morn-ing. "You look nice today. New hair?" She surveyed the topography of my chest; my cleavage was peeking out of my neckline. Things were getting baggier. My breasts were deflating, leaving storage space in the cups of my bra. It seemed such a wasted opportunity, like perhaps I could start carrying my wallet in one cup, my phone in the other. I could store nuts in there for winter. I needed to buy smaller pants. They were rolled at my waistband and held there with two safety pins that left impressions on my stomach when I undressed each night.

"No, I think I'm tired. Evelyn was screaming last night. She keeps seeing cats."

"Cats?"

"Yeah, cats. I guess. Unless that's a word for something else. I haven't figured it out yet. I've thought of making a guidebook: 'The Care and Feeding of Disappearing Minds.'" This was a mistake. I should have known better than to expect Marlene to laugh when there wasn't a laugh track.

"Like one of those foreign language books? The kind that tells you how to say 'Do you know how to get to the Eiffel Tower? Excuse me, waiter, are there nuts in this coffee?'" She smiled, her cheeks pushing up and almost covering her eyes.

I could almost like Marlene. Almost.

"Yeah, except instead of that, if they say 'Fuck the man too wise, please, Gracie?' you can go to the index and find out that they're saying 'Can you please give me some more salad?'"

"At least she is getting your name right and not calling you bitch or something." Marlene smiled with her lips pressed together. "Girl, you do not know what I've seen. Some kids, when their parents get the Alzheimer, are better off putting them in a home where people can watch them all the time, you know?"

"She doesn't have Alzheimer's. I told you this already. She's too young. The neurologist thinks it might be . . . a bacteria or fungus or something. They're doing tests and trying drugs."

Marlene squinched her lips together harder and said nothing. I turned to the refrigerator to find things for lunch that wouldn't make my stomach gurgle as it sorted the Good from the Not Good. My shirt slipped off my shoulder and I caught it and hiked it back up.

"Did you know that Iris Murdoch had Alzheimer's? And also E. B. White?" I asked, trying to defuse the situation.

"I don't even know who those people are."

I sighed. Marlene was still Marlene.

"Charles Bronson."

Marlene looked at me with wide eyes. "He's dead?"

"I don't know," I sniffed. "Maybe he's dead."

"Where did you learn that he has Alzheimer's?"

"In a pamphlet."

"He must be dead, since they don't know if you have it until the autopsy."

I threw a block of cheese and a microwave sandwich into my purse and walked out the door. "Maybe he's just seeing cats."

After work, I popped into a used clothing store. There was no reason to make a serious clothing investment on a temporary body, and summer was coming: I never wore shorts because of the travesty of my thigh cellulite, but Evelyn's study didn't have air-conditioning. I automatically went to my usual size on the rack and then remembered that I could slide east, counting down. I plucked a pair of linen trousers off the rack and held them to my waist. They looked like they'd fit and were only five dollars. Trying them on, however, they were as formfitting as grocery sacks. I giggled to myself. *Whoops, I need a smaller size!* I wanted to shout across the racks to every person in the store, the hipsters scouring the racks for ironic T-shirts, the retirees looking to stretch their fixed dollar. I wanted to call Marlene and tell her, just to feel the hate seethe through the phone.

I was a size I hadn't been since high school. When did this happen? Time was shifting backward. I needed to clear my head. I wandered over to the books. There's something very beautiful about the stuff no one wants anymore. You can hear the voices of the former owners floating in the air above the racks and racks of '80s prom dresses and '50s housedresses. When push comes to shove, the only thing that would be left of us in three hundred years would be our stuff. And not the stuff that you want to be remembered for, like your class ring or your school photographs. No. It would be anonymous stuff, like the Barbie Dream Date Game or the dresser where you hid your porn collection under your handkerchiefs and dress socks. The material dandruff keeps going, with or without us, it's the stuff that has permanence, even after it's been sent away on the Goodwill truck.

Evelyn's dementia pamphlet described how a moment from the past might seem like it just happened a few minutes ago. *The human brain has a great vault in which it stores every single moment, every utterance of your entire life.* What would a physical storeroom of every possession look like? Everything ever purchased, ever received under the Christmas tree or as a prize for pinning the tail on the donkey. There would be tables containing legions of goldfish, each swimming merrily in perpetual circles in their own little bowls. There might be an entire mile of clothes, hanging from smallest to tallest sizes, next to shelves upon shelves of every book I ever owned, including my baby book and *The Poky Little Puppy* and that tattered copy of *Are You There God? It's Me, Margaret* that I checked out of the library and then left accidentally on the bus and had to pay for out of my allowance. I was romanticizing things. Those goldfish would all be belly up and stinking.

My head started to feel swimmy. If it wasn't something greasy and delicious, I didn't want to waste a blue pill on it, so I chose not to eat, instead focusing on the sensation of my lurking collarbone. I spun on my heels and walked toward the door. A basket full of white gloves waved goodbye.

*   *   *

While Evelyn watched television, I fixed her evening tea. "Are you? Fuck that world," she replied, as though someone had asked her a question. Sometimes Evelyn got stuck on a word, using it for everything until it started to mean nothing and everything. This week, it was "world." Everything was the world. The world was everything. It made sense from that vantage point, but the previous week, it had been "wax," which had the bonus quality of being both a noun and a verb. I waxed her breakfast of wax and then had the wax to give her wax when she really wanted the world. World? Whirled. Whorled. Were Eld. Was she working her way through the dictionary? It was like the language of flowers, a song heard in a different lifetime. I tried to imagine her brain processes, the synapses getting stopped, road construction ahead, bridge out. There were plaques, apparently, clogging up the highways. I learned that in the pamphlet.

"Carla?"

"No, Evelyn. Aunt Carla is in Florida."

"Don't be ridiculous. I know that world."

"Do you want some tea?"

"Pinked?"

"Tea. Peppermint or chamomile. We're out of the blackberry. I think Marlene drank it."

"I just—"

I waited. Her face screwed up as she physically struggled through the fiber insulation in her brain, as though trying to remember a dream ten minutes after waking. I had a brief mental image of hitting her like a stuck jukebox, knocking free that aphasia, clearing out the Wernicke's area. There were moments when she was completely clear and then other moments when there was nothing, just nonsense.

"What, Evelyn?"

"I just . . . don't know where I'm going. I don't know where I just was and I don't know where I'm going right now." She pointed to her head, making the motion I remembered from childhood that meant she had a migraine and that I had to turn off all music, take the phone off the hook, muffling the sound of a busy tone with a pillow. "The—the world is hurting. My world."

Well, what can you say to that?

❉　　❉　　❉

"Grace. Move. Come up for air, Grace. Time to go to school, babycakes." A voice traveled from inside a cave, Evelyn's voice. She sounded like she was in a closet. Where was the light? My head hurt. My world.

I opened my eyes and then realized that I was on the floor of Evelyn's kitchen. Evelyn was leaning over me, with a glass of water and a handful of her own pills. When I moved my head, she shoved the pills into my mouth and then rubbed my throat, the way you would to get a dog to swallow heartworm medication. She looked at the glass of water then at me. I leaned over and spat the pills onto the floor, mentally calculating that I had just spit out $4.75 after insurance.

"You fainted. You haven't been eating enough. Look at your eyes. Sunken battleships. Carla, you should know better than to starve yourself."

"I'm not Carla." I groaned, trying to shake the swarm of bees from my head. I felt like I was going to throw up but knew already that there was nothing to throw up.

Evelyn rose, and for a minute, I flashed back twenty years to her standing at a podium, demanding equal pay for equal work, sun shining off her carefully mussed coif.

"Well, who the hell said you were?" She snorted and stepped like a pointe dancer through my sprawled legs, then glided toward the beckoning blue screen in the living room.

*   *   *

"Your mother found a mouse." Marlene was giving her nightly progress report on Evelyn's behavior.

"A mouse? In this house?"

Marlene eyed up the dirty corners of the kitchen, as though the likelihood of vermin inside was a very distinct possibility that she hadn't considered.

"No, outside. In front of the back door. She started crying. She was very upset. It was a real pain in the ass trying to get her into the house. She said it was her fault." Marlene always seemed to imply that Evelyn's fits were somehow in my control, as though perhaps I was putting Evelyn up to her hijinks, telling her to do strange things just to extract the most value out of Marlene. Put your panties on the outside of your clothes, I might have whispered to Evelyn at night. Insist on wearing a parka when it's 95 degrees.

"Are you saying that my mother killed the mouse?"

Marlene answered with her trademarked chuffling sound that

was my favorite of Marlene's nonverbal repertoire of grunts, snorts, and wheezes. I'd tried replicating the chuffle with my own cheeks, and it was much more difficult than it sounded. *Chuffle! chuffle!* There was a complicated sucking and blowing maneuver at work, but even then, I couldn't get the vibrato right. Perhaps my jowls were no longer meaty enough.

"It just died there, I guess."

Mice didn't just die out in the open like that. It must have been a cat, or perhaps a very tiny member of La Cosa Nostra leaving us a warning of some kind. I thought about saying so but then remembered it was Marlene.

She pulled on her coat and grabbed her plastic purse. "Did you pick up Ev's new meds?"

Ev!

"I did. Two at night, two in the morning, but only if she needs them because the pharmacist said that it will make her really sleepy, but it should cut down on the—the—uh, auditory hallucination type things. Which, you know, you might want to hit her with a dose before the kids start trick-or-treating tomorrow. That could go badly, otherwise."

"All righty!" She waved her hands to cut me off, as if I were wasting her time, and then headed down the backstairs and out the door.

I watched her through the window, veering away from and then toward her decrepit, dinged minivan. Ah, so the mouse was still there. Of course she didn't pick up the mouse. Of course not.

I went to the bathroom, headed to the study to change into my smallest pair of comfy pants, moved the safety pin in on the waistband with some satisfaction, and then headed to the kitchen to start dinner: a Swanson for Evelyn and a big bowl of salted watermelon for me. Evelyn was sitting in her usual place, her hands folded in her lap like a prim little girl. I headed into the kitchen to make dinner, but something about her expression made me turn back. Her hands weren't folded—they were holding something.

"What have you got there? Can I see?"

She thought about it for a second, looking at me warily. Then she showed me just the tail between her fingers.

"I'm going to need that." I leaned toward the garbage can, but Evelyn pulled away and then shoved the dead mouse between her legs and clamped her knees together.

"No! She's mine now. Fuck that world!"

I could feel the retch building inside my throat. My head felt light again, with the darkness closing around the corners of my eyesight, but I willed myself to stay in the present. I went into the kitchen, grabbed a small plastic container, and threw some paper towels into it. Evelyn had done the same thing for me when my hamster died when I was seven.

"What if she has her very own little bed? She can have a nap?"

Evelyn thought about it for a minute, then extracted the little corpse from between her legs and dropped it into the plastic container. It was surprisingly hefty for such a little thing, actually, like a small furry hand weight. Should we have a funeral? Did I need to download "Taps" from the internet to make it official? Or could I just put the tiny coffin on our front steps as a Halloween decoration?

Evelyn looked up at me, her eyes already filled with tears. Her hand reached toward me, and I moved to hold it, thinking of how she had held my hand during Chewy's funeral, how warm it had been on that sunny day, and how she placed a tiny wild violet between his paws before we gave his body back to the ground. I steeled myself to say something about how the lady mouse had had a good life and how we are honored to help her go back to the earth, but Evelyn's eyes flicked to the television and her outstretched hand found the television remote instead.

*   *   *

In the middle of December, Marlene called at 10:00 a.m.

"Is everything okay?"

"Everything's fine. She's watching *Toddlers & Tiaras* right now."

I rolled my eyes. Marlene started allowing Evelyn to watch the most atrocious crap, as though she no longer cared about my instructions or, perhaps, acted in spite of them. Things had changed between us. Now, when we saw each other in the morning, her eyes lingered over my emerging clavicle. Sometimes I rubbed my fingers against the prominent bone while talking to her, just to see her stare. She acted as though she had lost something or as though I had taken something from her. It made me want to laugh like a Disney villain. I desperately wanted her to call me a *skinny bitch*.

"I just wanted to remind you today's the day we start family care."

"Family care? I don't know what that means."

"It means that my hours have been reduced. I'm only coming for two hours a week. Today was my two hours for this week, so I'll see you next Monday." Marlene's voice was clipped and serious, the unfriendly way you speak when you fire someone or have to tell them that you backed your car over their dog.

"What? Are you serious?" My voice carried over the cubicle wall, filling the office. Keyboards stopped clacking as everyone eavesdropped. I knew they were doing it, because it was exactly what I did when coworkers were having arguments on the telephone.

"According to the paperwork that our office received, which you were also supposed to receive, Evelyn has been diagnosed with a long-term unspecific brain disorder. Her short-term illness plan only covers ninety days of in-home care. You've already gotten more than that just because it took so long to get the official diagnosis."

"That's not an actual diagnosis. That's a 'we don't have any fucking idea' diagnosis."

"Well, you should call the insurance company. They're the ones that pulled the money."

"Marlene. You can't leave. Let's be serious. Do you really think that Evelyn can take care of herself?"

"The idea is that our service gets the family up to speed, and then the family steps in."

"There is no one else. I'm an only child."

"Then, in those instances, there's always private care. Hospice, that kind of thing. You should call the insurance company." Marlene desperately wanted to get off the phone.

"I can't afford private care, and Evelyn isn't *dying*, Marlene! She can't go into hospice."

"You should call the insurance company. Sorry, they sent you the notice two weeks ago, it says here." Marlene's voice was a security door, bolted from the inside.

"I didn't see any notice. Marlene, please, don't. Don't go. We need you."

"Call the insurance company. Maybe they have another suggestion."

She hung up. Desperation lurched inside my empty stomach. Who could I get to babysit Evelyn? After five minutes of Googling church groups and in-home care nurses, which cost more than my actual take-home pay, I decided that if Marlene and Evelyn's doctor thought that Evelyn was fine by herself, I would trust in the system. Mostly because I didn't have a choice—meetings stacked upon meetings made that decision for me.

When I got to Evelyn's that evening, the entire house was dark. Walking through the kitchen, I noticed a bit of dirt on the floor, then footprints in the dirt. In the living room, there was a tremendous stain in the middle of Evelyn's cream carpet. From the smell, it could only be one unmentionable horror. The stain spread out, Evelyn's neat small footprints radiating out from it, as though she had paced in concentric circles through her own sorrowful poop explosion. My throat closed tightly, and I felt something rumble inside my chest as I realized that if the carpet looked like this, Evelyn would be worse.

The shower was still running, curtain open and towels everywhere. I stepped over damp, reeking towels. At least she'd known that she needed a shower.

I paused near Evelyn's bedroom door and listened to her erratic breathing sounds. She murmured something in her sleep. Dreaming again. It was easier to let her sleep and hope that she wasn't actually sleeping in her own shit. I wondered if her dreams were visual salads too. If there was a God, he made her capable, gave her an executive job or maybe made her the president and she was wearing a stunning Chanel suit and showing women how to change the world. Or change their heads. Whichever.

I wandered into the study and flopped onto the miserable futon. It reminded me of a toadstool. I was Alice in Wonderland and the Queen of Hearts was asleep in the next room. I wondered what size Evelyn had been in the 1960s? Maybe a six or an eight. The standards were different then. Women had hips. Evelyn's closet had boxes of vintage fashion, original Halstons, things she wore to Studio 54 in the early '80s. As a child, I had even loved her boring daywear—tailored cigarette skirts and adorable little cashmere sweaters. Soon. Soon. It was becoming a mantra. I concocted outfits from memory and slowly drifted off.

"Grace!"

I bolted off the futon, clattered through the hallway and into her room. She was sitting upright. She blinked at me twice. From the way the light glinted off her head, I could see that she must not have rinsed all the shampoo out of her hair..

"Are you okay?"

"The cats." She moaned and then started to cry.

"Oh, Evelyn," I sat next to her and put my arm around her back and was rewarded with a good crack across the face.

"I DON'T KNOW YOU! YOU DON'T TOUCH ME!"

I felt my lip to see if it was bleeding. "Muth Err, I'm Grace. Your daughter. Grace."

"You are not. Grace! Grace!" She yelled toward the open door and then wept harder. "Gracie! My little fat Gracie! She's at school. I know what. She comes home. I know that she does. Any minute."

"Evelyn, it's me. I'm Grace. Me. Grace is right here."

"You are a foul, lying bitch. You are not Grace. You are a harsh and brittle little shrew. My Grace! Where has my Grace gone? I have lost her. We are lost. The world."

She sank down onto my thigh, her fingers gripping my forearm so tightly I knew that it would bruise, and yet she wouldn't let go. Her sobs turned to hiccups and then the soft breaths of sleep. We sat that way, together in the dim room, picking through a mental warehouse and watching the world gradually disappear.

WHERE SHE WENT

BEFORE WE SHOWED HER THE UNNAMED BABY, SHE HAD BEEN A HAPPY woman.

Or at least she thought so. Sometimes, when she'd drive up the street of their desired bedroom community, she'd look at their little bungalow squatting in its wide corner lot and it would frighten her, how perfect and happy her life was. The windows with awnings were two sleepy hooded eyes; the front door was a yawning mouth. Although she would never admit it to anyone, some nights she paused for a moment in the driveway, afraid to step into its open jaws. Then she'd shake her head and think about the leg of lamb in her freezer and wonder when she was going to have enough courage to make it for dinner. She had never made lamb before, and she worried that she would screw it up by cooking it too long or not long enough or putting too much rosemary on it and the whole thing would taste like pine needles.

Once she got through the door, she would sit inside the front room without turning on the lights and listen to the wind howl. The glass in the old window frames rattled. Her husband, Carl, hated that sound. It was just a reminder of money flying out the window, he'd say, and then make a quick, slick motion with his hand, as though their money was very eager to flee on lubricated chutes. Carl bought weather stripping and spent Saturdays haunting the windowsills, a burning candle in his hand. She didn't say it, but she liked the rattling. It reminded her of the house she lived in as a child, with high ceilings and glass doorknobs and squeaky floorboards and a bathroom door that didn't close completely.

She and Carl were happy, it had been decided. There was no doubt that Carl was happy. He would often announce how happy they were, how lucky, how perfect and happy and lucky as they'd sit in their living room and watch television, each on opposite sides of the sofa with a pile of her furniture catalogs occupying the international waters between them. Certainly no one would argue with him about their happiness, their luck.

Normally, we keep our opinions to ourselves. On a whim, one evening we sent her a dream of a baby girl, with long eyelashes and big dark eyes even though the woman's eyes were blue. It was a strange dream for her, a very simple one. We normally doled her complex epics, comedies, or fantasies, with casts of thousands and subplots that wove into other subplots.

In this dream, she was bathing a child, only a few days old because the baby still had that blue umbilical cord piece stuck on her stomach, dark and solid as a crayon. She cupped the warm water and brought it over the baby's skin, taking care to keep her head out of the water. The plastic bathtub was light blue; the fluffy towel that she planned to wrap the baby in was pink and smelled of Dreft. She felt awkward holding this baby. She worried that it was too cold or that the baby would get sick. And then she woke and remembered that she was not a mother and there was no baby. It was a good dream.

That evening, while Carl read the newspaper, she sipped a glass of claret and flipped through a Restoration Hardware catalog. She kept thinking about the baby, wondering if Dr. Freud was happy now that she was apparently dreaming directly out of textbooks.

When she got up to use the bathroom, Carl asked where she was going. It was a ridiculous question, really. She snapped that she was going to the bathroom and perhaps he'd like to know how many squares of toilet paper she used too. He looked up at her, injured with eyebrows lifted, and then murmured that he was sorry to have taken an interest in her. She said nothing and left the room but was even more irritated when she returned. He always asked her where she was going. It was annoying. She wondered aloud why he always asked her that, even in the middle of the night, when the answer was always the same. He said nothing, but his eyebrows were working, knitting a suitable answer that would not upset her. She could tell. Finally, Carl folded the paper and reached up to her and murmured that he was afraid she would leave. He said this in a way that seemed to offer proof of how much he loved her. He watched her closely for a reaction.

She reached out and took his hands and kissed him softly, and then said nothing as his hands left hers, went to her hips, and pulled her closer to him. She was accustomed to this. Sometimes they would lie on their oversized sofa together; his hands would wander while he talked about ordinary things, such as what they should make for dinner or their plans for the weekend. It was as though he were not aware his hand patrolled her hips, an explorer looking for the perfect spot to plant a flag.

Then his tongue slicked out to touch her lips slightly, as though ringing a doorbell. She acquiesced. She always did. She had been with Carl for almost her entire life. She was thirty-four, and they had started dating when she was nineteen, so it had been certainly all her adult life and over half of the part of her life that mattered, the years between ages twelves and now. As she kissed Carl, she kept thinking back to his last comment, wondering if she should have just said *where would I go?*

Her hands never sought him out. This was not to say that she did not enjoy the things he could do with his body. She did, but she knew that he was always there, as ever present as a weather vane. She felt guilty that he enjoyed her body so much while she felt as though Carl's body was utilitarian. Solid. Warm and covered in a downy fur that seemed to thicken and multiply, staking new territory as the years passed. A body made for taking out the garbage and wearing denim. Carl's body seemed as ridiculous as the bodies of the fathers of her childhood friends, men who mowed lawns in cut-off business slacks. But Carl was not a father because she was not a mother.

She wondered what her alternate universe self was doing right then, if she were sitting in a sleepy-eyed bungalow like this one or if it were something entirely different. She wondered about Carl's alternate universe self. Did he have a mustache? Did he wear different cologne? Did he like onions?

In the next dream, we played a little trick. This time, we kept the baby out of it, but she was at the ob-gyn to have stitches removed.

Her doctor was happy and smiling and asked how the baby was, asked if she was able to get enough sleep, all the while combining the dull ache of having given birth with the sharp pinches as the stitches were removed. The doctor was her real doctor, a dog enthusiast, and in the examining room, there were pictures of his Weimaraners receiving ribbons and standing at attention on little pedestals. On the ceiling above the examination table, there was a poster of dog breeds, and to keep her mind from the pinching, she read them to herself in the same voice she imagined she used when she read to the nameless baby. Miniature Schnauzer. Whippet. Briard. Poodle.

Carl sensed that something was troubling her, so he suggested a trip, something to get away from the darkness of winter. He thought for a minute and then suggested the vineyards on the coast. Yes, walking through old buildings made of stone permeated with fermented smells. It was something that made her happy, and she could lose herself in the planning. He knew her well. She nodded and offered a weak smile. It was a lovely idea. They could come home with a few cases for summer entertaining in the gazebo, and it would give them an excuse to talk about the trip while they poured wine—without sounding like they were bragging, which was the most important thing. Yes, it was a good plan. Carl patted her on the shoulder and asked if they were out of coffee. She told him to add it to the shopping list.

In her dream that night, she took the baby grocery shopping. It was her favorite store, although she had never been inside it before, one with the crooked floorboards and the decadent cheese board and vivid fruit that seemed obscene in the middle of blustery January. Exactly the kind of store she would shop in—if she had any idea where it was. She strummed up and down the aisles, the cart humming like a zither on the wooden slats. The baby cooed at the colors and stared up at her as she shopped. While she was searching the shelves for Desitin, she recognized a boyfriend she'd dated in college before Carl. He was in the same aisle, debating various sticks of deodorant. She hadn't seen the man in years, but there he was, minus the dreadlocks and with new wrinkles under his eyes. His eyes slumped downward for a cursory glance at her body and then continued onward, pushing his cart full of pomegranates, tapenade, brioche, shrimp, and a bottle of pinot noir. The year on the bottle was 1997. In her own cart, a loaf of bread, diapers, formula, cans of soup, cheese, hamburger, and an envelope full of coupons. She laughed to herself and patted her receding baby tummy.

During the day, she found it difficult to concentrate. Sometimes she would feel a sense of panic. Who was watching the baby? But then she would remember—it was all just a dream.

Just a dream. As though dreams weren't important. We get that all the time.

She tried to fill her waking hours with projects. She dedicated herself to her collection of catalogs. Carl called it furniture porn, and in some ways, he was right. She flipped past the ones where the homeowner sits on the edge of a sofa cushion wearing a loud sweater and gardening clogs, as though they would much rather be pulling weeds. She liked the rooms with only furniture in them the best. She could easily imagine herself in those rooms, straightening the paintings on the wall or taking a book from the shelf. She did not mind being alone in her catalog world. There was not a question of talking about what she and Carl would do or not do. There was not the subtle play for more and more touching.

The next night, she found herself sitting on a sofa. Not the overstuffed sofa that sat in their bungalow but a different one, one covered with a blanket to protect it, or maybe to hide it. She rested the nameless baby on her legs and they just looked at each other. The baby gripped her finger and she softly stroked the loose skin of the baby's hand. There was a pink hand-knitted layette on the table, a personalized label inside that read *Hand stitched with love by AUNT DENISE*. She didn't have a sister.

It was the same baby every night. Her subconscious had provided us with a name although she could never quite recall it. It was an old name, beginning with a vowel. It was a name you might have seen on crumbling gravestones in churchyards. In the mornings, she knew it upon waking and would think herself stupid for having forgotten it, but then after ten minutes, it would be gone, as ephemeral as a sigh.

One night, we made it morning.

She walked into the little nursery, gathered the baby up into her arms, and smelled the crown of the baby's head. She could never get enough of the baby's smell, sweet and somehow also sour and a touch of her own smell as well. She brought the baby back into the master bedroom, which was not the bedroom she shared with Carl in the sleepy-eyed bungalow but rather an entirely different bedroom with high ceilings and Victorian moldings and cheery white wainscoting that had a shelf at eye level. On the shelf were little treasures—teacups and colored bottles and tiny rocks. She knew that it was her bedroom because it was exactly the bedroom she would have chosen for herself. She placed the baby on the bed between her and the sleeping form of a dark-haired, lanky male form. She did not look up from the baby, but she felt him turn over and whisper good morning. This was Carl? No. It could not be Carl. She could hear a smile in his voice. The warm sun was shining down on the three of them. She knew that it would wake her up, and they would be gone, leaving only her utilitarian husband in their place.

The next afternoon, she broached the subject of children with Carl. He responded that he was too selfish with his time and her attention and very simply did not want to complicate his life. She was surprised by his frankness but also completely not surprised. They had discussed this early on. Neither of them made enough money to pay for the house, their life, and a kid on top of it all. A kid, he said, and a baby goat is what she thought of at the time. He liked his free time. He liked her salary mingling with his, their zip code, their cars both parked in their double garage. Their house, their life, was made just for two. Somewhere in her certainty that nothing good could come from her choices, she hadn't dwelled on the issue, thinking that they would have broken up by the time it mattered.

She decided instead to think about what she would make for dinner. Perhaps she would attempt the lamb. No rosemary, though, she decided. She was too skeptical about the rosemary, and even though every recipe on the Internet declared it crucial to a successful lamb meal, it seemed as though you really weren't supposed to be eating it. It was an accidental spice. Or herb? Maybe it was an herb. She wasn't sure. She'd have to look that up somewhere. No. She could make the lamb however she wanted. Yes, with roasted root vegetables tossed with some imported olive oil that had cost $25 at an Italian market. While slicing the fennel, she decided that she needed to stop dreaming of the baby and the baby's father. She would just stop. Push them from her mind. Concentrate on what *really* mattered.

How quaint.

That evening, seated in their dining room with the Wright-inspired furniture, Carl declared the leg of lamb a success. She smiled and replied that she had had an epiphany. Carl made a joke about a Lamb of God and she laughed, even though it wasn't funny.

That night, we put her back into bed with the baby's father.

Her greedy hands explored his tall frame, and he whispered assurances that he would be gentle and that she should tell him immediately if anything hurt, but his mouth brushed up against her ear in such a way that she quivered, feeling heat rush through her body. She thought about making herself wake up, right then, but she did not want him to stop, wanted instead to weave herself around him, keep herself there in that place. After they were finished, she wanted to tell him that she was going away, that she would not see him or the baby again, but instead she rested her head against his smooth chest and listened to his heartbeat and the soft sounds of the baby girl from the baby monitor.

Before bedtime the next evening, she grimaced as she swallowed a plastic cup full of green Nyquil and then took another half dose, just to be sure.

We do not care for challenges. We sent her strange, terrifying dreams of penguins with teeth and women with white powdered faces chasing her through a maze of thorns.

For many nights after, she doggedly insisted on taking the sleeping aids, even still through months of vicious nightmares, until they became so bad that she could not even remember why she started taking Nyquil in the first place.

Sometimes even we are surprised, but we are also patient.

One evening in early summer, she used the last of the ropey liquid and did not open another bottle. The next night, she stood with the baby's father in a waiting room.

A door buzzed and a nurse in a mask came out and waved them in. A sign said INFANT WARD—ICU. Her baby was lying there in a small plastic bed that reminded her of an under-bed storage bin. The baby's once vivid eyes had gone dull and her skin was gray. She and her husband donned gowns decorated with ducks wearing sailing caps, muted green masks, and powdered latex gloves that smelled of talc. She wanted to hold the baby, but the wires and monitors made it impossible. There was a single pink teddy bear. She could only put one latex gloved hand onto her baby's little chest and feel the chilled flesh, despite the heat lamps that tried to keep her warm. The noises coming from the baby sounded like those of an old person, raspy air and congested wheezes. She knew that if something happened to the baby, she would not be able to go on, she would not be able to do anything. She would simply fall into a heap on the floor and never move until she died.

Somehow this might have been the father's fault, although she didn't know how that could be. He was idiotically chatting with the nurses about visiting hours, and she wanted to hit him. She wondered if maybe it was really her fault. She grabbed a Sharpie marker from the nurse's chart and inked the baby's name on the inside of her hand.

She heard the doctor telling the baby's father that the next twelve hours would be critical. She traced around the baby's belly button where just six months before there had been a withered blue cord toggle. She looked to the baby's face, waiting for a giggle, but the baby either could not or didn't want to.

In her head, she decided to make a deal with someone, anyone: just make the baby better and she would never wake up; she would continue to live here with her baby, whose name she couldn't remember, and the baby's father, whose name she never learned. Or if that weren't a good enough deal, then she would offer that she would just never wake up. She would be neither in her world nor this one. Just make the baby better. Just let the baby be okay. Just let the baby live.

As though we are in the business of striking bargains.

FUSE

THE FIRST THING MY SISTER DOES EVERY MORNING IS POKE ME IN MY RIGHT rib, which is her left rib, but if she pokes too close to her own heart, I don't feel it. Our legs are usually tangled in the sheets, my ankle bracelet beeping softly because it always needs charging when we get up. This morning, she won't talk to me, just like she hasn't talked to me in months, not since Justin Henry went away and broke her heart.

The rib poke is the only thing she still does from before Justin Henry, so I don't mind. Then we get up, take a shower, pee, floss our teeth. Olivia refuses to look at me while we perform our ablutions, turning her head away from the mirror and away from me, her other mirror. A picture of Justin Henry used to be tucked into the space just below the light above the medicine cabinet, the yellow beam shining down on him like he was a saint or the Pope or an astronaut. I took his picture down and tore it up. I feel a little bad about that, after everything that happened. I could have left her that one thing of his, I guess, but looking at it every morning and every night before bedtime put lead in the pit of my stomach. I tried telling Olivia that, but she screamed, "It's my stomach, Dahlia!" and you know, she's not wrong.

Before we lived here, we were in show business. When we were very young, before we could read, our uncle carried us on his back, in our little bunkhouse. We had to hide because otherwise no one would buy tickets if they saw us for free. We were the ODD sisters, Olivia and Dahlia Davis, O. D. D. But then our uncle got in trouble for driving drunk and maybe something else—hurting a lady?—and he had to go to jail, and we now have our friend Ashley, who tells us that we shouldn't call her Aunt Ashley because she's not our family or even our friend—she's court-appointed and watching after us is how she earns a living. Before Ashley, we had Aunt Theresa, and before her, Aunt Michelle, and before her, Aunt Connie, who smoked and only ever looked at our feet or our hands. They were all court-appointed, but Ashley is different: she's nice, she's our friend even though she's paid to do it. She has other cases, though, and only forty hours a week, so we see her just a few times a week when she drops off groceries and picks up the bills from the mail to pay them and give us an allowance. Otherwise, we can do whatever we want if we don't leave the house.

I miss our little bunkhouse that our uncle carried us around in, where we twisted together into each other, two legs, two arms, two faces, but we had gotten too big for it anyway. I wonder what happened to it.

We spend most of our days on the sofa watching Olivia's stories or out in the garden, which is what I prefer. The garden is just a patio and two buckets of dirt filled with plastic flowers, but I call it the garden. Olivia won't move her leg when she's being stubborn, and she's stronger than me, so I don't bother resisting or arguing. We sit on the couch, and I turn my face to the big bay window and let the sun bathe me in light while I watch the trucks on the road in front of our house. Or I read. I like reading stories about pirates and swashbuckling. I like it when a hero stops bad people from doing bad things. There's always a damsel in need of saving. Sometimes the hero carries her to safety, kind of the same way our uncle used to carry us but nicer. Olivia sometimes tells me that I'm breathing too loud, if my lungs inflate while hers deflate. It makes her mad when our breathing isn't in sync. I don't like it either, but I still do it. Our fused sternum is a barred cage.

Justin Henry liked me at first. I never liked him. Olivia liked him from the start. She always gave us hiccups when she saw him, and he said she hiccupped like a little bird or a mouse. He always used small language with Olivia because I guess most girls like to be thought of as little. He was too stupid to see that when you're only half a person, being small is the last thing you want. But Olivia didn't care. She ate it up. He was stupid and did a bad job shaving and his skin was always full of acne, even though he was also losing his hair. "How old is he even?" I'd ask. His breath smelled like the Flamin' Hot Cheetos he ate and then hers did too, and sometimes he touched our stomach when they were kissing, and once he put his hand on our zipper and reached down and then I screamed and fainted, and Olivia said I was a drama llama. At least he stopped that time.

I wish I could get a job driving a truck. There are a lot of truck drivers that pass our house, big clanking hunks of metal with so many wheels, the cab impossibly small compared to the payload dragged behind it—a hotel for objects, unlimited potential. I've watched videos and studied photos of the little cab interiors, a perfectly proportioned home that moves across the country, with room for two. I imagine myself wearing greasy overalls and loose T-shirts and sleeping snug inside the sleeper cabin. Commuters would only see my profile. To them, I would be the driver, solo, alone, even if it was Olivia doing the driving. She could sleep while I drove and I could sleep while she drove. We'd just need to learn to drive and then we could make our own money and no one would recognize us when we were working. Olivia said she was only humoring my truck driving idea, but then, after Justin Henry, she wouldn't even humor me anymore.

Sometimes Olivia falls asleep while we're watching TV, and I can usually find a good movie on the old movie channel. I look for Errol Flynn, Tarzan, and monster movies if I'm not too sad. Monster movies are the scariest when the mobs come for the monster. I used to hate monster movies, but I was watching them wrong. I always used to think Frankenstein's monster just wanted to touch the girl's face softly to prove he could be gentle and kind. But after Justin Henry, I was afraid for the sleeping girl. Now it feels good to think about carrying a pitchfork or a torch and crossing a moat to kill the beast because the beast is Justin Henry, and I will hurt him again and again.

Olivia used to play games by making rules for us. One day, we could only walk by counting each step; she was even and I was odd. Another day, we had to put our clothes on backward and speak sentences backward. Another time, we couldn't speak at all and pretended we were mute freaks. We carried two notebooks and two pens, hanging from cords around our necks. The cords kept getting tangled together, but it was fun because we aren't actually mute freaks so it was nice to know things could be worse.

Now whenever I suggest fun day rules, she changes the subject or says, "I don't feel like it."

Back when Justin Henry showed up, she taught him some of our games, even though I asked her not to. Those were our games only. And then he said, "Me Kiss" and "Me with live to you want I" and "You of care take me let" and "Everything ruins Dahlia. Her to listen don't, wrong is she" and "Me like doesn't Dahlia" and "You only love I" and then he spread our legs and she let him and I thought about monsters and truck drivers and torches and pitchforks and screams.

Olivia talks about separating us. Every time we go to the doctor's office, she asks about the operation. The answer is always the same: There has never been a successful separation of dicephalic parapagus twins. The only way doctors would attempt it is if one of us were dying. In the car on the way back to our apartment, Olivia whispers, "I'm dying" as she traces an invisible meridian down our torso, the part of us that is Olivia splitting away from the part of us that's me. "Snip snip snip, you're gone."

Ashley hears her and reminds us again that we're special, we're so unique, we're one in a billion.

I like Ashley a lot, but we're not one in a billion when there's two of us.

Magnets stick together like glue, but they also hate each other if you turn them around, pushing away from each other so hard you can't stick them together no matter how hard you try. I don't want to be separated from Olivia, but also, I wish we could be stuck together some times and then unstuck others, so she could go kiss boys and do whatever she wanted and maybe I could take driving lessons. I don't know what it would be like without Olivia. Fewer of her stupid daytime TV stories, I guess. Fewer games. No more backward sentences.

Olivia keeps insisting that she's dying, and I keep feeling like if one of us died, the other would die soon after anyway, even if they could separate us. I know I would die without Olivia. But maybe Olivia has a chance. Better than mine, I think. Maybe she'd go find Justin Henry. Maybe she'd sob or lie down on his grave, something I never let her do. Ashley says it's not a good idea anyway, his family might see us and complain to the authorities. The courts already let us go on a technicality, so better not give them a reason. We can't even sneak there because of my ankle bracelet. I don't think he's in a grave anyway. I think they burned him up.

Good.

Olivia wants me dead for what I did to her boyfriend, and I wanted him dead for what he did to me. Either both of us are right or neither of us are.

Sometimes I think we're already apart. Like there's a me that's out on the highway, driving a big rig that roars like a cannon, like a monster about to attack.

My face in the driver's side window is pristine. And to my right, a hollow space where Olivia once was, a ruffled bit of skin where she once resided. Our legs still work the pedals though, her arm and my arm tandem on the wheel. We're steering us toward a future without Justin Henry, without his face, his breath, his other parts forcing our parts to enjoy him. Just me, missing the part of us that is Olivia, aiming at the vanishing point that might be large enough for both of us.

LOWER MIDNIGHT

SOME BELIEVE THE WHOLE ISLAND IS HAUNTED, FROM STEM TO STERN, from the top of Lighthouse Hill to the bottom of Shubrick Point. The scientists assigned to the island tell me this on my third day, matter of fact, while we're anchored fifty feet off the Great Murre Cave, waiting for a white shark to come back and finish eating its freshly killed sea lion. One little haunted island is nothing compared to the constant ripping of flesh from bone just off the shore. It's a violent place. And, of course, there was that female skeleton found inside the cave, resting as though she'd stopped for a nap a hundred or maybe a thousand years ago. Out here on the water, the air smells like the dumpster of a Long John Silver's, and globs of blubber float serenely past my side of the boat. *I'm a scientist now, I work with real scientists, I was chosen because of my smarts, I belong here.* I have to keep reminding myself; I have to focus on this one-in-a-million opportunity. I'm floating in a tiny boat some hundred feet above barrels filled with nuclear waste sunk by the US Army in the '50s, and I'm supposed to be recording minutia about one of the world's greatest alpha predators for the marine biologists who hired me to do a real science job and will pay me money for it. Instead, I'm wondering if the woman from Great Murre Cave could be the lady's voice I heard in my room while trying to get back to sleep last night at 4:26 a.m.

The bed I sleep in is in a room at the top of the stairs and to the left. I'd call it "my bedroom," but it doesn't feel like mine. There are three other staffers sharing the room across the hall, and I thought it was nice that they gave me private accommodations, a welcoming gesture. In the '60s, an intern painted Barbarella on the inside of the bedroom door, and even though the homage had been mercifully painted over in an institutional brown in the '70s, everyone still called it the Jane room. Even the biologists who stayed in the Jane room call it "the Jane room," instead of "my room." It's just what you do. A hundred years ago, at least one of the lighthouse keeper's children died of diphtheria on the island. Probably not in the Jane room, the biologists all tell me, nodding.

What most people don't know about this island is that the Cassin's auklets burrow into the rocks. They don't know that right after sunset, those weird little seabirds come back from hunting and fill the island with a terrible roller coaster of sound. It's like a thousand lunatics getting high off helium and then screaming. Every night, I convince myself that sleep in the Jane room is impossible but then bolt wide-awake sometime later. The clock always says 4:26 a.m. The auklets are gone, and instead I hear the asthmatic rasps of a dying child in the Jane room. I mentally sing '70s sitcom theme songs because it's impossible to be afraid while humming the *Welcome Back, Kotter* intro song. Still, the room gets damp and cold, and I'm not sure if I'm hearing ethereal whispers or just the mice trying to dig through my duffel for the last of my PowerBars. I am a scientist,

I remind myself. It's the mice. Of course it's the mice. Everything can be measured, explained and quantified, including mice. It sounds like they are scritching out my name. This is just auditory pareidolia, I know this is true, where my smart brain is incorrectly interpreting the sounds into something with meaning. It's a Rorschach test for my ear. The whispers accuse me of not doing well enough in high school geometry, of being such a pretty face, of never really sitting up straight. And that's when I usually hear that lady's voice. Sadness. Ice water. I have a feeling of being strangled.

In the morning, over almond milk and Kashi, I laugh, telling my fellow scientists about the voice and the chill. I ask them which of the three across the hall has been hiding the smoker's hack. The DNR guy, who sleeps in a different house, asks me if I got stuck sleeping in "that damn Jane Fonda room" and then says simply, "Yup, that's why. Damned ghost."

That day in the boat, a twenty-foot white shark splashes us with her tail. In the spray, for just a moment, I swear I see a figure standing at the base of Great Murre Cave. This time, I don't say anything to my fellow scientists. No answer is a good answer. A fine answer in fact. I hum the Kotter theme song because it seems like the right thing to do.

At night, at 4:26 a.m., I look out the Jane room's window and see shapes fly past, white shapes that seem more liquid than bird. It must be a meteor shower, maybe trails of ionized particles shed and reflecting radio waves back down into light, sound, electrical interference. There is a high-pitched wheeze in the darkness, more urgent now than before, somewhere near the closet. Someone needs to get that poor baby to the doctor, I think, but where? Where? Outside, a face looks up at me. Aleutian features, maybe Ohlone tribe, hand-hewn clothing, shredded bark skirt, pre-Gold

Rush. She's beautiful and strange and she waves to me. I wave back and she smiles and dissolves into sea spray. The ghost baby coughs and whines and I say, "Shhh, I'm here, it's going to be okay. I'm a doctor and I won't let anything hurt you."

Maybe one of us believes it.

INGOB

WHEN CHIEF WENT MISSING, MOST OF THE TOWN THOUGHT MAYBE HE'D wandered off onto the ice and frozen to death. It wasn't unheard of. People had done it more than once in the long and storied past of Death's Door, particularly during the weak light of February, when the snow and cold and ice feel like a personal affront. And Chief was a funny kind of sort, the locals all agreed.

You could always tell when Chief was driving the county snowplow because everyone's mailboxes were all knocked askew. Chief thought it was hilarious stuff. The locals rigged their mailboxes on hinged arms so that when the plow hit it, the mailbox would swing out and then pop right back, like a screen door. A mailbox could last five, maybe six seasons on a good swing arm, but without one, that sucker would be lucky to last until Christmas. During the summer, you can always spot the houses of rich people from Chicago just by looking at their mailboxes—fancy hammered copper or hand-painted with loons and seagulls. You'd think the locals would have been mad at Chief for not being careful, for damaging the private property of people who paid their high waterfront property taxes, paid for the free school lunch program for the Door's kids, but the locals just kind of chuckled. Chief was doing what we all were thinking. A copper hammered mailbox, who had time for that much niceness on a damned mailbox? Chicago people, pretty much. Besides, waiting for these ornamental little boxes to take a fall, it was something to occupy the mind when everything went all white.

On the last day anyone saw Chief, he was waiting for me in the parking lot of the Sons of Bjorn and Daughters of Mis-no-quo-que Door County Tribal Recreation Center. The county snowplow growled way back in the distance, fresh from having plowed out the bingo hall and casino lots. In such weather, good parking spots were worth every additional yard saved walking to the building, so he parked out back near the tree line. Chief was a good guy.

The first thing I said to him that morning was, "That your handiwork in my drive this morning?" I had woken up early to dig myself out. The weatherman had forecasted a good four inches, but it was at least eight. I braced myself for a sore back, but when I trod out in my old roommate's Sorels, the snow had been cleared, leaving a neat little wall of snow next to my car for me to knock over when opening the door. There was a little joy in that moment, knocking that whisper bank over, but at the same time, it seemed a shame to sully such a nice plow job. For being so pure, snow sure makes a heavenly mess, but it's nice to look at at least.

It was Chief that had dug me out. He said, "Ain't nothing, Mabe. Plow's used to doing much bigger work than that, your little drive is no problem for her." It was a tremendous number of words from him, especially so early in the morning. I made a mental note that he anthropomorphized his plow like it was a horse and he was the rider. I added it to my mental file folder labeled CHIEF (NO COMMONLY KNOWN LAST NAME).

Together, we walked into the bingo hall, stamping the snow off our feet on the vestibule rug like chickens scratching in a yard. Chief held out a hanger and waited for me to take off my parka so that he could shelve it. I forgot to look at the temperature when I passed the digital clock at the bank, but it must have been negative something because Chief's boots were making that below-zero squeaky sound, like Styrofoam rubbing together. You'd think that winter would be quiet, without the Muffys and Tads beeping their Beamers at every little thing. And I suppose that it is quieter. But there are also sounds that can chill a person much more than the cold: I can hear the bay ice's groans and creaks from my bed at night, the moaning as the water rolls under the surface.

I just remembered, he also asked me if I was going to call.

"No, I'm the money today," I told him. Due to the gaming commission's rules, we can either pull the balls and call or we can sell cards and dole out prize money. I guess that's to keep everyone honest, but I've yet to see anyone hit the big time with a bingo heist.

The Sons of Bjorn and Daughters of Mis-no-quo-que Tribal Recreation Center is one of the few places in the Door Peninsula that's open year-round. Sometime in the '80s, a group of locals nabbed themselves an official Indian gaming center through a weird loophole that left everyone in Bemidji standing around with their mouths open, a bunch of blond Belgians claiming to have indigenous ancestry. The government contracts were rewritten right after that, which just goes to show that it's a good thing to be the first. Remember that.

Chief was known as the only actual Native American in Door County. His real name wasn't Chief—I found out by accident when he paid me for a bingo sheet. Saw it on his county ID, but I didn't share it. I don't talk much to the other locals, and they return the favor for the most part. I figure that the reward for being observant is getting these little jewels all to yourself. The Sons of Bjorn and Daughters of Mis-no-quo-que had tried and tried to get Chief to work for the casino. Maybe the bosses figured his dark skin and eyes added a little authenticity amid the sea of pale Northern complexions and saved them from having to tell the story of how a Native American tribe occupied a patch of land near Jacksonport for about nineteen months between 1805 and 1807. Just one woman stayed and married a Norse settler and had the typical brood of eight or twelve kids, half of them with dark hair and blue eyes, the other with blond hair and brown eyes. Genetics at play. In the long expanse of dark winter hours when there's no work, most residents of Death's Door like to do crafts. I read genetics studies. It's some fascinating stuff. You can't talk about that stuff with the locals over lingonberries at the diner though, unless you can break it down to counted cross-stitch samplers or something.

Chief and I never really said it out loud, but whenever we spotted each other, we tended to linger until interrupted. We might have stood together a few more minutes that day if the vestibule doors hadn't opened, hitting us with a blast of heat and cold as the two temperatures rushed in to fill the vacuum. That's when the tall man walked in wearing a long, dusty overcoat that was far too thin for the weather. You know how coats can take on a different feel when they're worn, as though you can almost sense the aura of their owner still clinging to the lining? This coat didn't feel like the tall gentleman, like maybe it didn't belong to him, like maybe he found it in the back of a car or maybe left behind in a lost and found box.

He had a black scarf pulled over his face, which wasn't odd in itself given the weather, but he had two different colored eyes, like you sometimes saw on dogs, one brown and one icy blue. There's a double helix that would have to happen to make such a striking pair of eyes. Sometimes it's a sign of Waardenburg syndrome, usually accompanied by weird patches of hair and hearing loss. I read that on Wikipedia, during a late-night research session on seemingly unconnected physical traits being linked to the very same genetic fluctuations. Fascinating thing.

I would have been a good geneticist maybe. If I had taken that scholarship to that school in California, or hell, even the UW, I think I would have figured out how to save babies or maybe flipped a switch inside the DNA strand to make you immune to AIDS.

"Bingo?" The stranger had a strange, somewhat feminine voice. I made a mental note to reread the Waardenburg entry on Wikipedia.

"Right in there, sir." I broke out my summertime tourist voice. "We're not quite open yet, but you can come in and warm yourself—"

He stomped his boots and then walked through the doors into the hall. Chief rustled inside his big county-issue coat and flexed his fingers. Chief's fingers fascinated me; they were something you'd see on a tree instead of a person, thick and rooted at the base, gnarled and tapered with half-moon nails shining off the tips.

That was another thing Chief said to me that day. He said, "Ya. I think I'll just watch today." I didn't think anything of this because I know that Chief liked hearing the numbers read more than he liked the possibility of winning the bingo wad. Once Chief had told my coworker in the blackjack pit, Nils, that he could see colors when people talked. Nils had replied that he was full of bullshit, but then a few days later, Nils asked me if I had heard about such a thing. I explained that it was really a thing called synesthesia where brains embellish one sense with another, have touch sensations with taste or hear sounds with visual colors. Having someone interested in my genetics hobby was a novelty, especially someone as good looking as Nils, so I indulged in a few more sentences than normal, explaining that it is a very rare neurological condition, affecting only about one in every twenty-seven thousand people. Nils chuckled and said, "Just what I thought. Bullshit." I felt a little guilty, like it was my fault for not explaining it good enough, like I didn't agree that Chief was maybe a little special. Like, I should have mentioned that sometimes on a slow shift, I noticed Chief had missed some called numbers on his card because he was just staring off into space. When I told him he had to pay better attention if he wanted to win, he replied "Sometimes, Mabe, the numbers just look so pretty."

They think Van Gogh heard music when he looked at his starry nights. Working at a bingo parlor, you get to believing in a one-in-a-million shot just as much as you doubt the rarity of a sure thing.

I only worked part-time at the bingo parlor because I needed something for the winter. The bingo gods wouldn't let me off in the summer to rake in the tips slinging wood-fired goat cheese and cherry pizzas to the rich people, so bingo had to be part-time, not full. During the summer, I mostly worked at D'Amico's, but like all the other restaurants, it didn't bother staying open past the tourist season. Half the locals call it "that Eye Talian place."

From a genetic standpoint, the townies were weaker than city people, breeding more cheap summer labor to man the ice cream parlors and clean the hotels, until that's all anyone here will be able to do, until everyone thrives under a four-month period of extreme activity followed by eight months of hibernation. Everyone told me I should have been in the group that was smart enough to leave. I probably should have been, but Aunt Sharon, who raised me, needed help at the pie store, so it seemed smart to wait a year, and then another year, and then came the strokes and things fell into place. As they do. It's funny how you can't see the moment in your life when everything changed until a decade or more down the road.

The tall gentleman had his coat on Doris's chair and had pushed a second chair into the spot we always left open for Bernard's wheelchair. The other bingo players elbowed each other and nodded toward the violation. During the summer, it was useless to maintain lucky seats because tourists have eminent domain by virtue of their exotic license plates. However, during winter, the locals rescinded their largess and took back what they considered theirs by birthright—from stools at Al Johnson's to preferred parking spots. I could already tell that this was going to be what we call in the bingo trade "a situation."

I went about my opening duties, counting out my cards and wads of singles, tens, and twenties. Chief took up his favorite position, a table that was equidistant between the coffee machine and the snack table, where Ida was kneading mashed potatoes into lefse dough for the lunchtime bingo.

I started the blower on the Bingo King and unwrapped the tray of freshly numbered Ping-Pong balls. We got new balls each twenty-four-hour period. It seemed like such a waste but was so ordered by our lord and masters at the gaming commission. Years ago, Carol from the nightshift would take the used balls home and fashion them into wreaths by spray-painting them gold and silver. Then, she sold them to the tourists for $34 each plus tax. I used to think that people who came to Door County were just rich and stupid, but then I went to Key West five years ago and spent $60 getting my hair braided with a bunch of little shells at the end of each strand.

Now I just think something comes over people on a vacation. We all have that brand of stupid embedded in our DNA somewhere.

Doris walked in and stopped short, giving the stranger a cocked eyebrow. She wriggled her stout body, as though gearing up for a fight, and then beelined to her usual chair, now occupied by the gentleman's black coat.

Doris cleared her throat, drawing the new guy's attention. He reminded me of a grackle, the way they delicately dip their heads to drink while bobbing around to watch what the other grackles are doing, never really concentrating on any one thing, one eye always following the action. He flapped his long hand at her, a spidery in-cantation with his fingers, and turned back to the bingo card menu. For a second, I could see the little girl Doris might have been half a century ago, sitting in the corner with wet underpants, scolded by an uncaring authority figure. It was a solid, clear picture, right there on her face. She spun on her heels and hurried to the opposite side of the hall to sit with the smokers. They regarded her like she had three heads but made room for her in their area just the same.

Chief was watching too. I shrugged at him and smiled. His brow creased and he went back to studying the tall gentleman.

The money shift was a fast ordeal. It's just you out there, mak-ing change in your head, playing tricks with numbers, addition and subtraction, carrying the one and then jockeying for singles through a field of raised wrinkled hands, blooming with green. Whenever I watch the money person from the calling tower, I always think they look like a fancy dancer, splays of colored bingo cards twirling in the air.

So, I got busy, juggling cards and special games, the Mega Bux and the Imperial Blackout, the Big X and the Dirty Dozens. The bingo hall was beginning to fill up with bodies and coats and wet

boots making squeaks against the linoleum, and I didn't even realize where I was on the floor until I was standing right in front of
the tall stranger. "What can I get you, sir?" I always reverted to my
waitress mentality. The formality was one of the reasons that the
regulars like me, I think.

"Give me one of everything." He looked up at me that time, his
strange eyes seeming to move independently, one slow and one
fast, as though he belonged to two different, separate wild animals.
Years ago, I'd read about the uncanny valley concept, an issue where
when humans looked at a very realistic recreation of a human, say a
robot or a baby doll, they would become uncomfortable, filled with
a sense of revulsion and dread. I'd never quite understood that fear
before. Certainly, we know that we are real and the wax figure or
animatronic mechanism is not, right? Yet, watching as the tall gentleman's face tried to work itself into something human, as the eyes
rallied to focus and the corners of his mouth twitched out of time, I
understood. It's not their unreality that is terrifying, it's ours.

"Everything." He handed me a fifty, seemingly withdrawn from
nowhere. That's it. He reminded me of a television magician, the
kind that claim they know how to levitate or encase themselves in
a block of ice for a week. His voice sounded like rustling leaves or
maybe a rusted chain dropping to the floor. And then his face was
just normal and somehow very appealing. I felt warm, like I had
just sipped the most delicious hot chocolate, the way it blossoms
in both your stomach and your brain at the same time. It was like
falling asleep in the backseat of your parents' car, knowing that the
best way to pass the time was to just sink into the darkness and be
rocked by the road.

His fifty was in my hand, but I didn't remember taking it from
him. I reached for my change belt, and in the process, I dropped

every carefully collated pack of bingo cards in a flurry of pink and blue and electric orange. Far across the bingo hall, Chief pushed his chair back, making a tremendous squeak, and he headed toward the coffee pot.

"Fuck!" I squatted to pick up the cards before the floor boss saw it on his camera. I'd have to get a new pack and then stay after my shift to reconcile the shuffled bundle if anyone saw the pack leave my possession.

"Now, Mabel, you shouldn't use such language." The gentleman chucked his hand under my chin and tilted my head up. He smiled and I saw exactly what it was that had sent Doris running: His eyes were somehow not there, the way a dead raccoon on the side of the road is both something and nothing, an empty place. He was a trickster, playing trickster games. Something elemental inside my nethers buckled. I had a feeling that if I said anything else, engaged him in any way, he'd get me to say something that I wouldn't mean, some kind of bad thing. I could feel the animal part of my brain light up, start hitting all switches on the "fight or flight" response. Sweat tickled my cheek.

"I'm sorry, sir, if I offended you."

"No, it's not me you have to worry about, darlin'. The good Lord doesn't approve." The skin of his hand had an odd texture, like a chameleon's, pebbly and room temperature.

I said nothing, racing against the likelihood that I'd hear Lars's squeaky crepe-soled shoes against the Congoleum bingo hall floor. The gentleman shifted in his seat, and I could picture how it looked on the security cameras, me kneeling at his feet in flat black-and-white videotape.

"You don't believe in the Lord Almighty, our Father who art in Heaven?" For a second, I thought he had asked me to wash his feet with my hair, but then I realized that he had not asked this, had not even said anything that could be confused with the words "feet" or "hair." I shook my head to erase such wild imaginings. Then he leaned toward me, so close I could only focus on either his dark eye or the arctic blue one, rimmed in black. He rubbed a lizard thumb against my lips, then let his hand drop.

"I can see that you are a nonbeliever, so I will offer you some divine inspiration. *Inspiratus* since you pride yourself on knowing how things came to be—from the Latin meaning *inflame* or *to inhale*. I prefer the fiery version myself." He raised his hand to my face and splayed his fingers. "Watch the first five balls called. You will then have your proof."

He turned to the darkened flasher board, as though expecting the first called number to appear at any moment. And with that, I was released. I would have died right then, just to know if his thumb tasted salty or sweet, but I fought the urge to run my tongue against my lips. The stranger's fifty was still crumpled between my thumb and forefinger, and I was still thinking about how looking into his chalky blue eye reminded me of the time I was climbing a barbed wire fence as a child and stuck my hand directly down onto a twist of sharpened wire. For a moment, there was no pain, just the sickening feeling of being trapped and irreversibly broken.

Chief had come over and was swiping up the fallen bingo cards. I didn't realize until that moment that I needed saving, but he pulled me to my feet and took the fifty from my hand and thrust it at the tall stranger. "Your money isn't good here. I think it's time for you to leave."

The strange gentleman slowly regarded Chief's six-foot-six, four hundred-plus pound body. His face features shuddered, eyes blinking out of concert with each other. He had lost interest in me and it was like a greenish swamp water light was shining directly on Chief. Chief planted his feet at shoulder width, as though gearing for a fight, and then somehow diminished with a slight shrug.

Then the gentleman smiled, gathered his coat and bingo menu as though it were his own idea, and slowly bundled back up. I could still feel the heat of his gaze against my cheek. I studied the buttons on Chief's county-issued snow parka and waited until I heard his footsteps get farther away.

I wanted to cry, the way you do when your car slips on a patch of black ice and does a sickening slide, and then suddenly, against all reason, you are able to right the car and drive on as normal. I managed a nod, which Chief returned. He looked across the floor and shrugged. Lars was already on his way over.

Chief said to me: "Sorry, Mabe." His words were oil and smoke. "I didn't notice at first, but when he started talking to ya, I saw it. There ain't nothing in there. If Lars yells at ya for the mess, you can tell him it was me." He zipped his big coat, buttoned the storm flap, put on his gloves, and walked out the door.

Lars was there, mouth already moving faster than his feet. "What is going on out here? What did you do to the pack?"

For the rest of my shift, I kept thinking winter thoughts: frozen pipes, tongues glued to flagpoles, and the ice fishermen on the bay, pulling a fish by its lip into a foreign, waterless nothing where its fins flex futilely against the air.

*　　*　　*

At the end of my shift, I had to count and recount my bingo card pack and then talk with the auditors as they watched the security tape to make sure no one had managed to pocket any cards. All the cards were still there. No bingo heist on the day that Chief went missing. It's all in the records, every form filed and signed in triple. When I left after all the extra paperwork, it was dark again, still dark it seemed, and for a moment, it felt like the day never happened. Especially because Chief's plow was still there, waiting in its courteous parking spot.

I asked them to let me watch the tape, wanting to see the exchange with the strange gentleman again, to see if it had really been only a minute or if it had taken the hours that it seemed. Lars said he'd see what he could do, but then Chief went missing, and it became police evidence. In fact, Chief's plow was still there three days later when the cops came looking for it and, by default, Chief. As far as the sheriff could tell, nothing in Chief's little bachelor's apartment had been disturbed since he left it that Wednesday morning. They studied "the incident tape," as they called it, the one that showed things from all angles, but from the gossip I heard in the break room from the auditors, the only thing it showed was me and Chief. The gentleman's face was always obscured, from every which way. In fact, he had somehow lucked into one of the only camera blind spots in the entire bingo hall. Somehow his face had become a blind spot in my brain too. I kept trying to pull it forward and came up empty, just a blurry shadow, a moving set of features belonging to the whole of humanity. The eyes, I remembered the eyes. I felt bad for not being much help, but Doris didn't even remember seeing the guy.

Naturally, the sheriff questioned me too, asked me about the tall gentleman, asked what he said and why Chief had stopped midway through filling his coffee cup to rush across the hall to help me pick up dropped bingo cards. They speculated that maybe the tall gentleman was my boyfriend and that we had a racket going. I admitted that it did seem odd, but really, they'd seen too many casino heist movies. In the process of the investigation, they found out that Chief was actually from New York and not Native American at all but rather Italian. Of course, they pronounced it *"Eye Talian."*

The one thing that I never told them, though, was the thing about the first five bingo balls that Nils pulled that morning. They were I 23, N 45, G 59, O 70, and B 3. I didn't write them down and normally wouldn't have remembered them at all, except that later, when Nils had asked me why I had to stay late and audit the dropped cards, I had told him the entire story. Then Nils had checked the session's history and looked it up. "Huh."

"See . . . nothing. The numbers are just numbers."

"Yeah. The numbers ain't shit. But the letters spell out 'In God.'"

"No they don't. They spell out 'IN GOB.'" I had twisted my face at him then.

"Maybe that's because there's no D in BINGO," he had laughed. "Or INGOB is something else?"

*   *   *

Eventually, there were missing posters about Chief in local gas stations and a reward offered by the county. The posters had his strange name that no one ever used. No one ever came forward with anything. I got called in to talk to the FBI in spring when the ice was shoving toward the shoreline. A jacket had washed up, county-issued and size 5XL, but there was no concrete proof that it belonged to Chief, no DNA evidence or any fingerprints. They eventually discounted the possibility that it was his because he would have had to throw it from a plane for his jacket to catch the open water in Lake Michigan. When I had read that in the newspaper, I got a chill, instantly picturing him flying through the air, captured in the talons of a giant grackle.

The posters withered and yellowed. Chief's picture took on an antique quality, and I knew no one really cared about Chief, they just wanted to solve the mystery. Everyone loves a mystery, especially when they don't know if the ending is sad or not. All of a sudden, people who never even uttered my name in their entire life were acting like my best friends. They all wanted to know the full story, firsthand. I obliged once or twice, but it felt like feeding hungry ducks—they only like you because you have corn. Then the posters disappeared, covered with fliers advertising trout boils and authentic Amish quilts and winery tours.

And once again, the lake and the bay crusted over, and now I am left to my space heaters and heavy socks. In the night, as I listen to the creaks of the ice, sometimes I imagine that I hear his economical phrases, hear him say "Mabe."

There's a new plow driver now, who fills the base of my driveway with heavy sodden ice chunks and takes care not to destroy mailboxes. The summer people will undoubtedly approve. No one would ever dare say anything, but we're all a little disappointed.

The winter is barren, so stark that it is easy to imagine that this time and place have slipped away and we are ageless and without technology. Chief and I, we don't belong here and never did, and nature had naturally selected its own. I know that if he hadn't stepped in, it would have been my casino employee badge picture staring out from the curling missing posters, me without even so much as a memorial service.

There is nothing for him even now, just a weak sun and a quiet clearing and a landscape that is open and without comment. When I pass the leafless trees, it feels like I'm being watched. There's a birch standing like a ghost among a grove of hickories, with their furry, frayed bark and gnarled limbs binding them to the here and now. I spend a lot of time walking through that grove and decided that the birch should be his memorial. Now when I pass by, I can feel the hair on the back of my neck stiffen, and I think I must have it pretty right.

PASSERIDAE

THE ROYAL EXPERIENCE CAST MEMBER HANDBOOK AND PROCEDURE GUIDE
recommends that if there is a natural catastrophe of any kind (e.g.,
hurricanes, tidal waves, icebergs) that cast members of Royal Experience Cruises are to remain as calm as possible to prevent likely
hysterics or potential rioting among the passengers.

It started when we heard an unfamiliar voice on the PA system
requesting that all hands report to the bridge immediately. The
voice had a thick accent. *The Royal Experience Cast Member Handbook and Procedure Guide* requires that all announcements made
over the PA be made by employees with either a neutral—British
or Norwegian—accent, and so even at that early juncture, we knew
something was wrong.

Shortly after the strange announcement, we all heard the captain asking someone to spare his life on the PA, followed by silence,
then an alarm, and then nine bursts of gunfire over a period of approximately forty-five minutes. This was what sent us out of our

cabins and into the laundry-folding closet. We have all come from lands with civil war and recognize these sounds. It traverses speech, but you listen to the instinct to hide.

David from India, whose real name is Venkat Raja, relayed to us a very depressing anecdote about the band on the Titanic who played music for the passengers until water was lapping at the soles of their shoes. We all joked to ourselves, about the number of crew who survived the Titanic (24 percent of the Titanic's total crew survived, a percentage point lower than the poor passengers locked in the below decks of the Royal Experience Cruise. We have since confirmed these numbers to be accurate. As well, none of the surviving crew members were musicians, a fact which was relayed to us by Oscar, whose real name is Jesús. No one in the laundry-folding closet was a musician by trade, although Michael, whose real name is Shridhar, could sing the theme song from the movie *Jodhpur Jovialities* in a manner that was very convincing and moving to us all, as the movie is about pirates, and we all felt deeply for the main character's plight as a cabin boy, all of us but Oscar/Jesús, who had not seen this film. A shame. Everyone in the closet had seen the movie *Titanic*.) *The Royal Experience Cast Member Handbook and Procedure Guide* does address icebergs but says nothing about terrorists, which is admittedly a striking omission in this day and age, but hiding in the laundry-folding closet, the hospitality team all had come to the agreement that terrorists are at least as dangerous as icebergs.

Rebuilding the scenes from the movie in our head, we envisioned how we could surge forth with the rest of the Royal Experience cast members, the housekeeping staff plus Usiku from Entertainment. We imagined there were similar groups of survivors, the engine room workers below, entertainers clustered under the crawl space in the stage outside of the atrium. We tried tapping out an SOS on the pipes and waited to hear a response, but the silent return was like the inside of a conch shell, somehow both quiet and a roar. From this silence, we came to an agreement that the deck workers—the traditional sailors that made our vessel go from one beautiful location to the next—must have sadly passed on. We said words of respect in our native languages, which between the eight of us totaled fourteen gods and six words meaning "grace."

In our heads, we constructed our noble deaths, heartwarming movie clips of our lives, grainy pictures borrowed by family members for a touching montage. We knew there would be a cinematic tribute, at least one if not more, and we each selected the Hollywood actor who would play us. Michael is always a showboat and wanted Keanu Reeves while Alex/Arivindan and John/Usiku both selected Oscar Isaac as their theatrical double. They hadn't spoken directly to the other since the disagreement, but later, Alex mentioned that he had written his will on the back of a dry-cleaning receipt and asked Oscar/Jesús to witness the signing, as Oscar had the most sonorous and beautiful speaking voice. Oscar then read the line from Arivindan's will that requested the producers of any film depicting the dramatic events aboard the Majesty of the Seas should seek Mr. Isaac for the role of Arivindan Ganesha Rathmanajami. Oscar then announced that Dwayne Johnson would play the role of Jesús Jaime Escobar, and we all had to admit that this was a pretty good choice. We all wished to change our selections and give them permanence, but there was only the one dry-cleaning receipt. We don't know where it ended up.

This is what happened: We did not have the 07:15 bell on the second day, so we knew that something was amiss, but we continued with our daily routines in the absence of the deck crew. What other choice was there, in light of *The Royal Experience Cast Member Handbook and Procedure Guide*? And quite honestly, we had more trepidations about the passengers than any suspicion about the crew's disappearance because this particular voyage's manifest had a strange ratio of demographics.

Normally, we counted on a moderate percentage of senior citizens and families mixed with empty nests and corporate outings, but this was mostly kids fresh out of college with their first real-world paychecks, making them feel secure enough to deserve a four-day weekend at sea, a cruise out beyond the international waters so they could spend money in our duty-free shop, then back to Long Beach, California, all in time to get to work on Monday morning a little sunburned and a little haggard from all the rum. The "party barge" these young travelers were fond of calling our vessel. This was not their parents' cruise ship, after all, as a new Royal Experience ad campaign assured them, over the background soundtrack of "Wet Ass Pussy," which was enough to repulse the baby boomers and their families. However, some white hairs braved forth, addicted to low fares and shallow promises of swimming with stingrays. On this voyage, the cruise to nowhere, we had already been alerted to the fact that 99 percent of our passengers were under the age of thirty and about half of them were under the age of twenty-four. An alarming proportion of youngs.

On Thursday night, the first night out to sea, the eleventh and twelfth decks' pools looked like a television commercial for a popular energy drink. John/Usiku reported that when he simply crossed over the promenade, he saw the bare breasts of at least four different women and Other Michael had witnessed a sexual act behind the statue of Neptune. Tom/Manicka relayed that out of a manifest that topped two thousand, his breakfast crew had only fourteen guests in the entire Magellan dining room and two instances of vomit. During a non-hurricane voyage, a one to seven ratio is very high for vomiting in the main dining room. Oscar/Jesús shared that after the first night, the hospitality manager issued a notice that all bartending staff were to under-pour the drinks, an order directly from the captain.

Indeed, on Saturday morning, the passengers returned to the pools and hot tubs, recommenced their waving for drinks, hands up in the air like they just didn't care. They had shouted this, the not caring, at Other Michael and his peers, causing Oscar to grumble they would care enough if they got tequila instead of vodka, or no booze at all, how would they like that? The executives of the Royal Experience Cruise Lines must have been very happy about hitting this sweet spot of passengers. A single passenger usually pays fifty dollars less for their passage than it costs to host them, so our goal was to ensure they spent at least one hundred dollars while on board the vessel, be it on wine at dinner or chocolate-covered strawberries delivered to their room or an attractive piece of artwork for their dens back home. Many of us in the laundry-folding closet rose to our positions based solely upon our talents for the upsell. At eleven to fourteen dollars per alcoholic beverage, it was not a difficult proposition, certainly, but not everyone can be as smooth as those on the hospitality teams.

The day's events were as follows: The bar staff ran out of commemorative Royal Experience shot glasses at 11:00 on Saturday morning. The medical officers were seen responding to a call on the bridge, and no one noticed that they had not returned until a girl stepped on a broken Tom Collins glass and needed a shard extracted from between two toes. She was taken behind the sushi bar by two pool waiters, and we assume someone did the needful. Other

Michael reported that the managers and bosses had been watching over the proceedings with stern visages but then stepped away from their posts sometime before 18:00 to report to the happy hour in Crustacean's Cove lounge on Deck Seven. Around 17:00, Arivindan's team of room attendants reported that the ship's air conditioners seemed to be malfunctioning, but his calls to the engine room went unanswered. The entertainment director led everyone through "The Electric Slide," which caused a fistfight to break out between two men with the odd coincidence of both being named Chet. Filling out the incident report took longer than normal due to this confusion. Other Michael signed this report himself when he realized that he was the senior member of the pool staff in the area. The passengers chose to eat at the Buffet of Enchantment rather than eat the filet mignon and lobster in the Magellan dining room, which was stifling and an entire elevator ride away from the pool decks. A near riot broke out when the hungry masses exhausted the supply of cheese teasers and buffalo drummies. It was a bad evening all around.

Attempts to contact managers on their communicators at 19:30 were unsuccessful. As the sun sank into the ocean, Venkat scanned across the waving arms and muscled backs and watched as the fore bartender craned his neck toward a darkened doorway, then rushed through it as though to avert a crisis. The bartender did not return, and soon, the front beverage station was overrun by boys in colorful swim trunks, trying to spin bottles of rum over their heads and impress the girls in bikinis.

When the door to the laundry-folding room opened for the first time, our first thoughts were of our supervisors catching us in the act of being cowards. Our second thoughts were of the terrorists and the violence we would most surely face, but when we aimed our flashlights into the intruder's face, it was just a woman passenger.

Other Michael put down his can of spray starch, and Oscar set down his corkscrew. (When he was not manning the pool bar with Other Michael, Oscar worked in the Schooner Bar on the fifth floor, off the solarium, so his corkscrew was always at hand for those too good for the umbrella drink.) The musicians from the Titanic were in our minds as we fought back the urge to ask her if she would like a nice rum runner or perhaps another pillow.

She squinted in the light of our torches, and in concert, we directed them at the floor, at her feet, at her unpolished toenails. We saw a thousand times ten passengers' toenails throughout the voyages, all shiny like polished red apples and adorned with an artistic rendering of flowers or insects or sometimes pink with the tips a single white line, as though grains of sand would not dare to get trapped beneath the nail. Already, she was unlike every other woman passenger on this ship.

We each exchanged looks and confirmed that she was not one of our passengers, did not sit at our tables nor occupy our roster of cabins, had not been waited upon by any of us, so we couldn't address her by name as we were instructed to do by the "Hospitality and Care of Passengers" section of *The Royal Experience Cast Member Handbook and Procedure Guide*.

"Can we help you, Miss? Are you lost? Do you need assistance getting back to your cabin?" Michael/Shridhar was the first of us to be able to speak.

"Hi," she said and then sank down onto a stack of clean pool towels. This was how we came to be introduced to Anne. It was by then our tenth hour in the closet.

We offered her water, some blankets, a guest robe, and half of a peanut butter bar that Alex had not even told the rest of us about. She refused everything, so one of us gave her a flashlight, and Oscar handed her a spare set of keys from his trouser pocket. The keys, he explained, could unlock closets and cupboards in areas we could not reach from our hiding place in the bowels of the ship, not without traversing dangerous areas that David/Venkat had reported might be patrolled by the intruders. Oscar explained that she could hold the ring in her palm and then lace each key between her fingers, creating a set of spikes that could be used to rake against an attacker's face. He did not need it because with his corkscrew, complete with an inch-long foil cutting knife, he was the best armed of us all. He could afford to be generous.

We would not admit it among each other, but each man was pleased to have her in our midst, even though our close quarters already meant that we had spent the previous hours in a dreamless half sleep, crushed up against legs and feet on either side, which was preferable, we had all agreed, to accidentally snuggling up to a cohabitant as a man would to a wife. We had calculated how many hours were ticking down on the back of the door with a cake of hardened laundry detergent. Thirty-seven hours before the boat was supposed to leave its anchored position forty-five miles off the coast of Ensenada, Mexico, another three until entering US Coastal Waters, another four before pulling up to the dock, which meant that we would spend at least one more night asleep in this closet.

In the back of our minds, we thought about sleep. With her in the room, the sleeping arrangements would be even more sticky. How could we sleep without touching her, a magnet to our hands, a strict violation of *The Royal Experience Cast Member Handbook and Procedure Guide* chapter on guest management. We were each feeling protective of her and yet oddly aroused by the proximity to a passenger. We could have overpowered her—how inappropriate it was to be with her in her sleeping garments—but here she trusted us. We were happy to have her. We were no longer hiding if we were protecting.

She looked down at her gifts and nodded, then sighed, a crumpling kind of sigh that made many of us want to punch the intruders and some of us want to punch the man standing next to him.

Other Michael extracted his courtesy card that would usually be placed inside of his cabins on pillows or next to the bar. The card read, MY NAME IS MICHAEL I AM FROM MALAWI. PLEASE LET ME KNOW HOW TO MAKE YOUR VACATION DELIGHTFUL ON ROYAL EXPERIENCE CRUISES. The rest of us followed suit, handing her our table tents and courtesy cards. Venkat quickly conjured an anteater out of three clean hand towels and then placed his card in the snout.

"Please, Anne, tell us what brings you to our humble closet?" Tom/Manicka asked. He was a head waiter and has achieved a complete adaptation of the flat American accent. He was admired by us all, except perhaps Oscar, who uttered ". . . puñal . . ." under his breath.

"I followed him," she nodded to Venkat. "There's no one left, anyway," she stiffened.

We all looked to Venkat, who didn't say anything and caressed the ragged edge of a blanket as though he was extremely pleasured by this movement. He had chanced a trip out of the closet for some bottled waters. He reported that he had heard sounds coming from some of the cabins on Deck Two, terrible wet sounds, voices moist as the earth, and sped back to report that he had not been seen by anyone.

"I said not to leave, puto. Chica saw, how many others you think spotted you, eh?" Oscar/Jesús said.

Venkat said nothing. Manicka shrugged. "Please, let us make peace. Mistakes were made, but we have a guest now."

"Can't you hear the announcements down here?" She fanned through the hospitality cards in her hand, impossible to read in the light of our misdirected torches.

Since the first odd announcement, we had heard mumblings through the PA system, but without opening the door, we could not understand what they were saying. The laundry-folding closet door had no lock, and if the intruders were in the laundry wing of the "Crew Only" hold, a cracked door and our bobbing torches would be very visible immediately, and so we felt that a lack of movement was our best defense.

"My friend Melissa is with them, I think. Those men." We waited for her to continue, but she again pulled back.

"They took your friend, Miss? Do you know where they took her?"

Miss Anne looked around the room wildly, looking at each of us in succession as though we are children. "Everyone. Everyone's gone. I don't know where. I just found you. That's all. The thing I can't puzzle out is what they're doing. Terrorists don't split up all the pretty girls from the rest of everyone and send them down to Deck Two to—to—for—I think they were going to be taken off the boat." She hiccupped, and for a second her face faded, then she swallowed the words back into herself. We wanted to know what was happening on Deck Two although we could wait. Many of us have seen this before, seen the silence where once the voices of sisters and daughters filled. These aches and truths come out later, as many of our secrets had in the previous ten hours.

"Pardon, Miss," Oscar said in a tone that was so strange and unrecognizable it surprised all of us. "I don't think they are actually terrorists. Terrorists would have blown up the boat by now, flown a plane into it or something? These aren't terrorists, Miss Anne. They might just be pirates, nothing more." He patted her hand, and we were all shocked by his boldness and envious at the same time.

Anne stared into a corner of the closet. We watched her face in the near darkness and were aware of how the air in the closet had changed. Where before there was the sharp smell of industrial laundry detergent tinged with our own aroma of sweat and cardamom (which seemed to mostly emanate from Shridhar), now there was a note of lavender and sweet milk, a fragrance wafting from the folds of her soft gray sleep clothes. Later, after everything was over, when we talked about this moment, we all agreed that we wanted so badly to bury our noses into the space between her pillowy breasts and inhale deeply. David confessed that he was most overcome not by the scent but rather the idea of rubbing his cheek against her stomach, feeling enveloped by her femininity and the way her cotton shirt would catch slightly against his five-o'clock shadow.

Oscar continued, "The way I'm thinking, they're going to do whatever it is they're going to do and move fast. Then they have to be gone, because at 06:30 on Monday morning, the owner of this cruise line is going to wonder why their boat isn't showing up in Long Beach, and I am thinking that someone is probably wondering why no one is answering the communication with the port anyway, so it might even be sooner than that. These guys are up on the bridge, they know the itinerary. So, if everyone's gone, then maybe they are too. We must keep hiding, señorita, wait here until day after this one at most. Not so hard, eh?"

"I need some air." Anne stood, still clutching the anteater made from twisted towels.

Manicka rose from a shelf full of sheets and placed himself in front of the door. "I'm afraid, Miss Anne, that I cannot let you put yourself in danger. These are desperate men, and we will protect you."

She smiled. "They're not in these passages. I didn't see anyone. You," she glanced down at the card in the anteater's snout, "David. You've been out. Did you see anyone?"

"No, Miss Anne," Venkat said.

"You forget something: if they're not terrorists, if they're pirates as you say—although the name makes me think of men in plumed hats with swords rather than semi-automatic weapons—then they are only taking what they want. They had their chance with me before and—" Here she shrugged again.

"Did you see them?" David tightened his grasp on his light, focusing it on her thigh.

"One, just. He was just normal. Like . . . normal. But with a gun. He made everyone go to the theater, and then he sent the pretty girls one way, and then later, the men, all the men, were sent the other way, leaving me with some old women who are still probably sitting up in the auditorium, waiting to be told what to do." We all exchanged looks with the other and each man pressed his lips together to say no more.

"When I crossed the promenade deck, I saw a sparrow. So, we can't be too far away from shore, right?" she asked with a single raised eyebrow.

We did not have the heart to tell her about the scores of nests tucked in lifeboats and riggings. What do the birds think, when they are at sea? When one moment they saw land, and suddenly, they were in Mexico or Jamaica or Alaska. It must be a shock.

"There are lifeboats. They're huge, though. I tried to get one down, but I'm not strong enough." She sniffed and looked into that darkened corner, addressing it as though it were a man. "I'm not the type of girl who walks away from these things, you know? Women like me, we're casualties, not survivors. That's got to mean something, right? It's got to mean that I'm supposed to make it out of this, you know? Like it's my . . ."

Here she smiled. In the darkness, we were transfixed. We wanted to lift up our voices and sing songs to her in our own language. We wanted to give her a new name, whisper it into her ear, gather up her muddy blond hair in a crown atop her head and make her into a princess. In the space of ten minutes, we loved her so angrily that we were without words. In the back, Alex sobbed and Usiku cleared a thickened throat.

"So I need help launching the lifeboat. I can get help to come rescue us, but you have to help me first." With this, she looked at each one of us, but none of us could meet her gaze save for Oscar.

The rest of us tried to stop her, reminded her of the math, the number of hours left, pled with her to wait, wait with us, let us tell her stories. We were not performers, but perhaps she would allow us the honor of being her entertainment. We did not want her to go. We wanted to cover her with our burgundy Royal Experience uniforms, wanted to hold her close within our laundry-folding closet and scavenge for her tiny bottles of gin and lukewarm sauvignon blanc.

Except that we did or said none of these things. We knew that we should have spoken against her and not a man among us could bring himself to do the needful.

We dutifully followed her up to Deck Seven, her bare feet making no sound on the thick carpeting of the stairs. We were aware for the first time in weeks, if not months, of the boat rocking in the waves like a needle skipping along a warped record album. We were spinning at 33⅓ revolutions toward something inescapable, and she stood at the middle of us all, turning, turning.

Each of us knew how to unshackle the lifeboat from its mooring, as it is a part of Royal Experience Cruises' basic safety training chapter in *The Royal Experience Cast Member Experience and Procedure Guide*. White as a storybook whale in the moonlight, the name MAJ-ESTY OF THE SEAS was printed in letters on the side, and we knew it was stamped on every ration tin and life vest inside the boat itself. It takes only two able men to launch a Royal Experience lifeboat, but all of us unlocked the crane and unleashed the cover while she stood against the deck wall to steady herself against the rocking. When the boat lowered to the level of the railing, Usiku unlocked the gate and gallantly stretched his hand to take hers. Each Royal Experience lifeboat can hold a hundred passengers, but like those launched from the Titanic years ago, Boat Fourteen would be pitifully undermanned. Alex took her other hand and together they guided her between rows of twenty-foot-long oars. At least two men must be left behind to lower the boat six stories to the inky ocean below, but Oscar jumped the railing and straddled a bench next to Anne and then motioned for the rest of us to lower the two of them down. So, we did.

We remained behind for a reason that even now we can't explain, but at the time, it seemed proper, chivalrous, like world-class customer experience.

It was night, deep and dark and alone. The bioluminescent jellyfish glowed just below the surface, marking their path to sea. We were uncertain which way was California and which was Hawaii; we did not know the elements of seafaring, only knew that the stars sparkled and the moon was bright. The Milky Way showed in perfect cross section, and from below, we heard Oscar explain to Anne which stars were important to Cortés and Pizarro. We listened without speaking. In the dark, we knew that the sound of gunfire made your mouth taste metallic, and we waited for the sound. As the lifeboat penetrated the waves, we yearned to reach out and grab the moon jellies and construct for each other glowing pink life preservers, lash ourselves with the stinging tentacles and drift away through a red tide toward Baja.

We did not return to the laundry folding closet. Instead, we made a single file line and with our right hands holding the brass rail, we walked up nine flights of plush carpeted stairs to the pool deck to see their departure better. In the light of the moon, we saw each pool had been overcome by a coral reef. Without thinking, Manicka flipped on his torch, and we saw the other Royal Experience cast members clustered together beneath the water, linked by chains, their pale limbs swirling like anemone. We recognized our friends, headwaiters and porters, pool boys and cabaret singers, each with whorled barnacles for fingertips. Over the starboard side, we expected to see a pirate boat, but there was none. In its place, a minefield of life vests, beacons blinking in the night, all drifting toward Bali or San Diego. We were musicians without instruments. We each picked a deck chair, sat down, and waited for an audience.

TEXTS FROM BEYOND

"Hi, my husband's texts aren't coming through right."

Another one of these. We get about 15 percent of our calls from customers who were having problems with their TFB—text messages from beyond the grave.

"How long has your husband been deceased, ma'am?"

"Fifteen years. I just got this phone so that I could talk to him. I don't know what I'm not doing right." Her voice was sweet, hinting of fairy tales and oatmeal cookies.

Fluid Tel's official script for call center agents was to remind the customer that it can take some time for individual loved ones to get through and then offer to upsell them on a more "comprehensive" text package, one that offered unlimited text messaging so that when the dead did start to send text messages, the customer would be able to focus on their reunion through Fluid Tel's network, which was the best coverage in the country, without worrying about being charged per text message. Customers usually never understood that they got charged for text messages that they sent *and* the ones that they received, which was usually what tipped them over the edge.

Her profile had come up automatically through the ticketing system when she dialed in. It included her address—an apartment number in a sketchy part of town—and her payment history, detailing that we always received payment within seven days of the bill being sent. Dorothy Zabrowski had only owned a cell phone for eighteen months and one of my quota-driven coworkers had already set her up with a plan that gave her a whopping 14,000 text messages per month, what we referred to as the PToDD (pre-teen or drug dealer) plan. I could see Dorothy pulling a stamp out of a dispenser that might have been from her dead husband's desk, her apartment punctuated with small reminders of their life together.

Her voice needed to be reading aloud about big bad wolves and houses made of candy. Life's cruel joke probably meant she had never had any kids with Darryl. I wanted to ask, to make it seem like Fluid Tel cared about her life, like she mattered.

"You're doing everything right, ma'am. I looked at your text service and it's crystal clear, no hurdles to Darryl sending texts. Did he have any hobbies when he was with us?"

A soft chuckle that might have been girlish sixty years ago. "Oh, Darryl'd spend all November out in the woods with our dog, Snickers, looking for deer. Only got a buck once or twice, but I think all that outdoor air was good for him."

"He might be up in the best hunting grounds you can imagine with Snickers right now. Time doesn't move the same way up there."

Darryl had probably never texted in his life. TFB always came from people who used their smartphones like a second mouth, people who might have had some essence of themselves trapped in the ether already. Scientists didn't know why it happened. Tests were still being done, secret messages whispered to dying techno-loving patients were dutifully responded to hours after death but sometimes not at all. But the truth was this: Even if you could resurrect Darryl and give him an iPhone, he wouldn't even be able to turn it on, much less figure out how to transverse the wiring of the inter-nether to send a note to his beloved Dorothy.

"I'm going to prioritize your text service so that when he's able to get to a phone, his message will be first in our queue to go through."

"Oh really? Would you do that?" She sounded happy. It made me happy, a little bit. Apparently, that was still possible. Maybe the damp ache hadn't completely taken over.

"Absolutely, ma'am, you're one of our best customers, and this is a service that's reserved for our top-tier clients." My voice might have sounded cheerful to anyone who didn't know better, like Dorothy. Maybe she bought it.

"Oh well, I'm nothing special, but that's very kind of you." She bought it.

"You're special to us, ma'am." I moused over to her rate plan and bumped it down to a level 1, the entry-level plan that didn't use much data and charged per text message. "We also have a special going on this month for customers who haven't yet gotten a text message from their loved ones. This should help reduce your monthly bill." I ticked a box on her profile "Has Been Contacted via TFB" so that she'd be less likely to get thrown onto the list of commissioned salespeople calling to upsell.

"Oh my! Thank you! I'm on a fixed income, so every little bit helps. Do you think he'll text? He never sent me love notes while we were married."

"I'm sure of it. Thank you for your call."

I ended early and put my status on "Make Busy" so that my next call would bump to another representative. Human Resources told me to bounce any TFB calls to coworkers. Apparently, that's a new process when an employee experiences a loss.

I hated that phrase. *Experienced a loss.*

Like if I looked hard enough, I might find my wife, Kassie, somewhere. Perhaps she's in the laundry room? Maybe in the basement, hidden behind the Christmas ornaments? I might pop down there and say, "Baby! I've been looking everywhere!" and Kassie'd chide me for my piss-poor attempt at wrapping the light strings when we took the tree down in January. Maybe she'd have found Violet down there too, overlooked, busily constructing a dollhouse out of a storage box.

I guess I'm just the kind of guy who keeps losing stuff. My daughter. My wife.

I should have taken time off for bereavement, but I couldn't afford not to work. The payments for Violet's surgeries were crucial; insurance had paid most of it, but we— I —still owed $8K on the deductible plus the funeral expenses.

We bought three plots—one for Violet and one for each of us. Such a tiny bit of land, who knew it could cost so much? It had to be a hundred dollars per square inch. We had picked out a beautiful white marble headstone, but the price for engraving was ridiculous. Who buys a stone without words on it? We did. The thought of Violet sitting there under a nameless tombstone. We can engrave later, bit by bit, first her beautiful name and then her birthday and then a reminder to future generations that this little girl was loved by parents too stupid to watch this miracle in light-up tennis shoes every precious second of her child-sized life.

One day, after Violet was gone, Kassie got a text message from an unknown number. It was an emoji of a lady dancing.

Who is this? Kassie wrote back.

Baby carriage emoji, the texter replied back.

Kassie ignored it. Then two days later: Baby carriage. Purple flower.

I grabbed Kassie's phone and typed in *Go to hell. Stop texting us or we'll report you for cyberstalking.*

In response, an emoji of a monkey.

"Monkey" had, of course, been the nickname we always called Violet. The next day, another monkey. Then a hot fudge sundae.

The day of the accident, Violet had been begging for a hot fudge sundae. Okay, but what kid doesn't beg for a hot fudge sundae?

We hadn't mentioned hot fudge sundaes in the house, where our smart thermostat might have been eavesdropping (A common conspiracy theory: our smart devices constantly listening for their own trigger word were actually spying and giving Big Brother data to help influence our voting patterns). Kassie and I couldn't bear to talk about Violet at all, really, after the accident, so there's no way Big Brother might have known about the sundae, so Kassie reasoned it really must be Violet sending the messages.

Kassie never wondered why the texts started coming. Some people thought the TFB were a form of control by a dark arm of the government. Other people thought a foreign government was trying to control our minds or get us to commit suicide. Some people thought they were doing it because they wanted to distract us from the dead male sex worker found in the hotel room rented by the Republican Party's presidential candidate. Headshock, they called it, using everyone's collective grief to control us, keep us distracted. If that was the plan, it was working. Election Day came (and the guy got elected, even with the dead prostitute headlines—"a triumph for gay rights," they had spun it) but we were still getting the texts.

Well, I never got one. Kassie did, though, lots of them.

After the hot fudge sundae came another dancing lady emoji. Then a man. Then an ambulance. Then a dove.

Violet knew how to text because she'd played with our phones, teethed on them, knew what magic was captured there in those black, unblinking screens.

The phone wouldn't stop. It was dropping coins in the wishing well of our brains. Violet was speaking to Kassie. Violet was over there, but she could still reach us.

Heart, we texted back together. Then a purple flower.

Princess with brown hair, it texted back.

Cat with a big tear.

Red car.

Ambulance.

Church with a heart over it.

Kassie stared at the phone. "The funeral. She remembers the funeral."

I didn't say anything. Neither did my phone. Violet wanted her mom, that's all it was, Kassie consoled me. I nodded, tight-lipped. My phone was useless, a brick to hurl into the empty sky.

Then Kassie's phone went silent for a few days. She panicked. Then she got a picture of a monkey holding its hands over its mouth. Speak no evil.

"Someone's telling her not to say anything. Come on, asshole." Kassie screamed at the ceiling.

Family, Kassie would text back every hour.

Family.

Heart.

Purple flower.

Family. Heart. Monkey. Family. Family. Heart. Girl with blonde hair.

Kassie stopped working because she didn't want to miss a text. We didn't dare tell our parents about the TFB. They would demand that I "fix" their phones so that Violet would start talking to them too. Like grandparents had some kind of first spot in line to talk to their dead grandchildren. Their kids were still alive, they had no idea what we were experiencing. Kassie took screenshots daily and emailed them to herself, to me, afraid that somehow these whispers would be gone the next time she looked at the phone.

*   *   *

Kassie never even considered that it could be me logging into the backend of the GUI at work, plugging her phone number in, and sending her that first message of the lady dancing. Be happy, dancing lady. I might have thought Violet would want her mom to be happy. Be happy and dance again. I'm sorry about the hot fudge sundae. I'm sorry that I turned my back for a minute. I'm sorry that our little girl was lost. Hear me now. I don't even remember what I was thinking. Maybe it was simple. Listen. We are still a family. Our heart is a purple flower. We are still a family. Come back to me.

The worst part of it all was that each time, for just a moment, I would forget that I had sent the emoji. For a moment, it would appear and then our girl would be alive again, be not lost. Our girl was there. And then I'd remember I'd sent the texts.

But then there came a text I didn't send.

I stopped after the baby carriage and the purple flower. Have another baby, I was trying to say. Violet would want that. But those tiny pictures were pulling Kassie away instead of giving her closure.

It was all she could think about, all she could see. So, I stopped. Purple flower. Violet signing off.

Then, out of nowhere, came the monkey holding its hands over its mouth.

That wasn't me, I wanted to tell her. That really was Violet. Or the government. Or someone at Fluid Tel logging into the backend GUI. But it was probably Violet, texting from somewhere, texting us from hell or heaven or from underneath the lawn furniture in the basement or from somewhere inside our hearts, willing her to be in the room with us. It was Violet. And it was real.

But I couldn't explain that. I couldn't tell my wife that it really was Violet's spirit, that some kind of insane magical event had happened because Kassie believed it had been so all along.

She didn't understand that it was our dead daughter telling me to stop being her mouth. Stop toying with her mom. Stop before it was too late. But I lost Kassie anyway. Lost her in the Fluid Tel employee handbook metaphor and lost her in the real world meaning, but not in that order.

She was recovered against the rocks on the beach, two weeks after she'd gone missing. My truest heart. The one person in the world that allowed me to create something wonderful for the first time in my life. My terrible fingers had caused her to leave, the same ones that had typed a dancing lady into a black, lidless eye. The same terrible fingers that had twitched when I got a notification on my phone while walking out to the street with Violet. Someone had mentioned me on Twitter. I turned my face for just a second. Just a second.

Then screaming, mine and hers and then Kassie's, an ambulance, a hospital, so many tubes, Violet's beautiful hair shaved and replaced by a web of scars, but all the money in the world couldn't save our girl, and when they unplugged the machine that breathed for her and when Kassie and I said goodbye, I turned my face again.

And now, Kassie knows. She understands everything. That's why she isn't texting me. Confused face emoji. Not because she couldn't. Because she knew what I had done to Violet. To her.

Face with open mouth and cold sweat.

Face screaming.

*   *   *

Dorothy's Daryl, on the other hand, would never send a message. He just wouldn't know how. I went into the backend GUI and typed in Dorothy's number.

"I only get one message, darling, so here it is. I'm here watching you. I love you. Be happy and don't come too soon. I got Snickers here with me keeping me company. Keep me alive down there as long as you can my love. – D" Dog face. Smiling face. Relieved face.

I set it to be delivered in two days.

Then I put my own phone number in and set the text to be delivered in forty-eight days. Maybe I'd forget I sent it. Even if just for a moment.

Two hearts. Smiling face with halo. Bride with veil. Raising both hands in celebration.

It would be good. Just for a moment. It would be good and it would be worth it.

Confused face.

Weary face.

Weary face.

Family.

FLARBY

DARBY WALKED CAREFULLY OVER THE SIDEWALK, WATCHING OUT FOR cracks and suicidal worms from last night's rain. Step on a crack and break your mother's back. She didn't want to do that; she was a good girl. Today, she had three weeks' allowance burning up inside her school uniform's pocket and she wanted a candy bracelet more than anything. And maybe a candy lipstick, too.

Ahead, three boys walked slowly, poking their way to school. Darby measured her steps, as she didn't want to accidentally catch up with them. She knew that if they kept up at that pace, they would make her late for school. Darby felt hate for them burn in her cheeks. She wouldn't, no, couldn't, pass them, though, because they would make fun of her, which was worse than being late for school. They were probably talking about her right now. Even if they didn't realize she was a mere one hundred feet behind them.

Darby felt the coins in her pocket, cool and steely. She held them in her hand. Her secret strength. They grew wet and warm.

She wanted to put them in her mouth and suck on them but didn't because of germs.

The boys wouldn't matter once she got to the Corner Mart. They'd keep going, and she'd go into the store, down the candy aisle, and get whatever she wanted. And then she'd feel good. Then she'd have won. She'd have won over all the kids at school who made fun of her. She'd have won over her parents who put her on a stupid diet. She'd have won over that lunch lady who came up to her at hot lunch and took her red Jell-O cake with whipped cream frosting away from her, even though all the other kids got one, because her mother had told everyone at the PTA that Darby was on a strict diet. The room mother had said that loudly. Everyone near her had looked at her, to see what she had done wrong to get her Jell-O cake taken away. But Darby hadn't done anything wrong other than being herself.

Darby quickened her pace. The boys were passing the Corner Mart now, and soon she'd be there too. Darby broke into a sweat and realized that she had to go to the bathroom. Well, she'd just have to hold it until she got to school, even though she was pretty sure it was both number one and number two. Some kids said the words "poop" and "pee," but Darby never said those words. She wouldn't even say "hell" when they recited bible passages in religion class, even though the teachers let you say it when you were talking about God. She wanted to be perfect. She knew that parents and God didn't love you if you were not perfect. She knew that she wasn't perfect on the outside, but didn't they always say, "It's what's on the inside that counts." Still, it didn't seem to.

Darby got to the store, and, for a brief moment, saw her entire reflection in the glass doors: big chubby cheeks; little pin-hole eyes; long blonde hair that didn't seem as long as it really was when compared to the width of her body; a polyester blouse that didn't quite fit right, stretched across her stomach; a burgundy school jacket that was tight across the shoulders and the back; fleshy knees that peeked out from beneath the pleated skirt hem. Her knees were the worst part. She hated the way they dimpled and the skin folded over them. She wanted bony knees, like Kelly Katzer's or Jacey Weidman's. They had pretty knees, not fat knees. Why did she have to have such ugly knees?

She wished that she could wear pants like the boys could. They didn't even have to buy whole uniforms. They could just wear black or navy dress pants and a white dress shirt with the blue school ties and blazers. They were the lucky ones. They didn't have to go to the uniform place with their moms, where Mrs. Lund (who had gone to Our Lady of Perpetual Sorrow, too) worked and get measured and weighed right in the middle of the store and have Mrs. Lund shout out the numbers to her stock boy, who was actually a man. And then, when they couldn't find one that fit her, as if Catholic girls were all the same size and could never be chubby, Mrs. Lund had just kept shaking her head with her arms crossed over her hard bosom and saying in her high-pitched voice which buzzed like a fly, "I just don't know what we're going to do about this." Her mother gazed upward, like the portrait of the Virgin Mary that hung in the school hallway, and shook her head saying, "Don't look at me, I certainly don't shove the food down her throat." Mrs. Lund had to special order a uniform, but it didn't arrive in time, so on the first day, Darby had to wear her church blouse with a blue skirt that was straight, not pleated like the uniforms, and Jacey Weidman made fun of her. Then, when the special ordered uniform did come in, it was still too small and gaped open at the bosom, which she for some reason had already. Next year, Darby hoped that she wouldn't have to worry, because sixth graders changed uniforms to the same ones the high school wore, so maybe then there'd be a size that fit her and Mrs. Lund wouldn't act like Darby was her greatest torturer.

Darby stepped into the corner store and walked right by old Mrs. Creepy without looking at her. She didn't like the way that Mrs. Creepy normally glared at her, it made her feel guilty for just being alive. It was as if she expected Darby to swallow up the entire store. Sometimes, though, she felt as if it were possible that she could. And, more secretly, sometimes she even felt like she wanted to, too.

She felt for her quarter, three dimes, five nickels, and five pennies. Still there, of course. She didn't plan to spend it all on candy. There was a barrette at Leibman's that she wanted to get her mother for her birthday next week. It cost fifty-five cents plus tax, so that only left twenty-nine cents for her to spend on herself. Her mom would like the barrette. It would look pretty in her pretty long hair. Her mom would be happy then. She would try it on and then say how pretty it was. Then maybe she'd say how pretty Darby's hair was and how it was just like her own. Then maybe she'd forgive Darby for not being pretty everywhere else.

Darby sucked in her stomach as she passed the news rack. If she wasn't careful, her skirt or her jacket would brush up against the papers and draw Mrs. Creepy's attention to the fact that she couldn't even go through an aisle without touching both sides as normal people could.

She stopped at the candy shelf. She liked to look at all the candy. They were so bright and colorful, all blues and reds and exclamation points. It was almost as good as looking at breakfast cereal boxes. She picked up the candy bracelet and looked at the price:

five cents. She put it back. She knew she'd end up taking the candy bracelet anyway, but she liked to linger over each and every candy and think about how they would taste in her mouth, and about how she was getting something that she shouldn't have. She liked the candy bracelets and necklaces the best because she could hide them and eat them one piece at a time and it could take up to a week to finish them if she ate them slowly.

The bell above the door rang as someone entered the store. Darby continued to look at the candy. Chocolate went too fast. She liked the jawbreakers a little, but they were so big that they hurt her mouth until they were halfway gone. The taffy was good, but it also went too fast. She picked up a big candy ruby ring and looked at it on her finger. The plastic ring part squeezed the flesh on the underside of her finger, but the candy gem looked nice, all big and red and shiny under the crinkly plastic cellophane.

Someone walked over to the comic aisle. Darby froze. It was Georgie Kopilanski, a sixth grader. Darby thought that he was probably getting some comic books to read in between the pages of his religion book. She had heard that some boys did that. And there she was, getting candy, probably the worst possible thing for a girl like her to be seen doing.

She ran into the freezer aisle and peeked around the corner. She didn't think that he had seen her, he was too occupied with Superman. She turned back to the freezers, wishing she could disappear. That bathroom feeling came back full force. She crossed her legs and jumped up and down a bit. She began twisting her body around. There was no way to keep it back anymore, she'd have to ask Mrs. Creepy if she could use the bathroom. But first she'd have to go past Georgie.

She walked down the aisle as quietly as she could. Think graceful, think Kelly Katzer. But Kelly Katzer wouldn't have this problem. Kelly Katzer would probably have started talking to Georgie; she could have probably gotten him to buy her candy.

Georgie looked up. For a second, his eyebrows went up as if he remembered her and was happy to see her, but then a look of disgust crossed his face as he remembered who she was. Darby's heart sank. Here it comes. Ignore him. Just ignore him.

Georgie stuck his tongue out at Darby.

"Darby, Darby, big fat Flarby," he chanted quietly, in a whisper so that Mrs. Creepy couldn't hear. Grown-ups weren't supposed to hear the cruelties of children. If they did, they might punish the bad child. But Darby knew that they sometimes really heard and pretended that they didn't hear. It was as if they thought certain children deserved those bad words. Mrs. Creepy hated Darby—she wouldn't care if Georgie kicked Darby or pulled down her skirt again, right in the store.

Darby turned around without looking at him and went back to the freezer aisle. A warm, thin stream of urine traveled down her leg. Darby pretended that it hadn't happened. She couldn't even think about it.

Fat. She was fat. That was a bad word in Darby's book. She couldn't even bring herself to think of the word. It was even worse than "hell" or "poop." He had called her big and fat. She hated Georgie. Hated her name. Hated her mother for giving her such a stupid name that made people want to make fun of her.

Mrs. Creepy could see her from the counter. She looked up at Darby, wondering what a kid was doing in the freezer aisle, probably. Most kids stayed in the comics and candy aisle. So, Darby pretended to study the contents of the freezer so that Mrs. Creepy would stop looking at her. Hmmm, frozen peas, corn niblets, frozen bread dough, she pondered as if she were a real shopper. The cold swirled around her bare legs, making the urge to go to the bathroom unbearable. She had to go *so so so* bad, but she couldn't because of stupid Georgie.

She saw Georgie finally go up to the counter, pay for his comics, and leave. She really had to go to the bathroom now, it was all that she could think about. She was getting chills and cramps from it.

Darby walked back to the candy aisle. She wouldn't be able to look at everything, just grab what she wanted, use the bathroom, and run to school.

"You know, you shouldn't eat that junk," Mrs. Creepy barked.

"Huh?" Darby jumped. She hadn't expected Mrs. Creepy to start talking to her. Mrs. Creepy never talked to kids, just told them how much money they owed for stuff.

"I said that you shouldn't be eating that junk. A big girl like you's already had too many sweets." Mrs. Creepy just held her tight little smile, as if she had just saved Darby from a fate worse than death. A fat worse than death.

Darby stood there with her mouth open. She didn't know what to say. She felt like crying right then and there. She felt like telling Mrs. Creepy that she didn't eat many sweets at all, that she wasn't allowed to eat any sweets ever, and that she just didn't know why everyone thought they were doing her such a big favor by making her feel awful about it.

"Umm . . . I've got to get something for my mother. She's having a dinner . . . a, dinner party, for her friends." It was a lie and lying was a sin. Her mother didn't have dinner parties, not ever, but Darby knew that TV parents gave parties for their friends. Her mother wasn't like those parents at all, but Darby liked to pretend that she was and tell other people that she was too.

Darby ran back to the freezer section. What should she get? What would be good for a dinner party? She saw a frozen banana cream pie. That sounded rich and fancy. Darby opened the freezer door. The coldness hit her bare legs and immediately she was sure that if she didn't get to the bathroom RIGHT NOW, she was going to have an accident.

She grabbed the pie and wiggled up to the counter as well as she could while holding her legs together.

Mrs. Creepy looked down at the pie and snorted. She reached down and picked up her pack of cigarettes. She slowly pulled one out with her thin, bony fingers that were the same width as the cigarettes, and put it in her wrinkled, lipsticked mouth. It was hot in the store. The sun was bright and caught millions of little dust flecks. Mrs. Creepy sighed and then she rang up Darby's purchases.

"It's for my mother," Darby repeated. "Dinner party."

Peering over the counter, Mrs. Creepy regarded her. "Seventy-two cents!"

You don't have to shout, Darby thought.

Darby plunked all of her money on the counter, and Mrs. Creepy picked out what she wanted with slender disgust. Darby would have counted it herself, but she was crazy with urgency, feeling that she would dirty herself at any moment.

"Do you want a bag?" Mrs. Creepy rasped.

"No, Mrs. Crigi, thank you," Darby said as politely as she could. "Do you have a bathroom I could use, please?"

Mrs. Creepy leaned over the counter and looked her up and down. Darby could almost see her thoughts, imagining Darby using the store's bathroom, putting her butt on the same toilet seat that Mrs. Creepy's butt sat on. Fat germs. Darby germs. She was going to say no, Darby thought, because what good would it do to be nice?

There was nothing in it for her. She wanted Darby out of the store as fast as Darby's chubby knees could carry her.

"Not for public use!" Mrs. Creepy finally squawked, slapping her bone and skin hand down on the Formica countertop.

Darby grabbed the pie and started toward the glass doors.

"Hey. You forgot something!"

Leave now. Get out. The pee was threatening to escape.

"Hey, Fatty!"

Darby stopped cold.

"You forgot your change!"

"Um . . . you can keep it." Darby knew that her bladder would burst right then and there if she turned and went back into the store.

Mrs. Creepy shook her head instead of saying "Thank you."

Darby left the store. Tears were streaming down her face. Don't think about it. It didn't happen. No, she wouldn't cry. She wouldn't cry!

Her bladder hurt. She was sweating despite the cool autumn breeze.

A little bit came out. She just couldn't hold it any longer. When she felt the warmth on her legs—a disappointment, a failure—more came out. Wet through her underwear, down into her socks and shoes. She started to cry more. The harder she cried, the harder she went.

Darby ran behind the store, behind the dumpster, and squatted there in the bushes where Mrs. Creepy couldn't see her. She was late for school, wet through to her skin, and now she was dirty from the grass and mud too. She stopped crying and looked at her frozen banana cream pie. She had almost forgotten that there wasn't really a dinner party and that it was a lie. What had she bought that pie for? Now she spent all of her money. Just because she had wanted to prove Old Creepy wrong, she had wrecked her mom's birthday present. Now, she wouldn't be able to buy the pretty barrette to give to her mom on her birthday morning. Now her mom wouldn't smile at her and say thank you and tell her what a pretty gift it was. Now she wouldn't put it in her pretty hair that was just like Darby's. Now she wouldn't say what pretty hair Darby had too.

Stupid pie. Stupid Georgie. Stupid old lady. Stupid Darby. Too stupid to even do something so simple as to buy her mom a birthday present. Georgie was right. She was a big, fat Flarby. She should have known that she would mess things up. What her mom always said was right: Darby always wrecked things, she couldn't do anything right.

She opened the pie box. The pie would have been good at a dinner party, she thought, with its pretty designs in the whipped cream. She imagined sitting at a fancy table with a white lace tablecloth and glittering silver candlesticks and forks and spoons.

A pretty lady would come in wearing an apron, like the TV moms do, and she would smile at Darby. She would be Darby's mom. "Darby, sweetie, would you like a piece of pie before dinner? Sometimes it is very hard to wait on an empty stomach for your daddy to get home," TV mom would say, as she would slice up the pretty pie and set a large piece on a pretty plate.

"Yes, please," Darby said out loud as she reached into the frozen pie with her fingers and broke off a chunk. She daintily bit a piece of the crust and cream and tasted it, with an expression of content like on the commercials, and said, "Oh, it's delicious!"

"I'm glad you like it, Darby, because I made it especially for you!" TV mom would say.

Darby shoved the piece into her mouth, not feeling how it froze her teeth. The cream melted slowly against her tongue. She imagined how wonderful it would be to die drowning in whipped cream.

"Oh, look! Daddy's home!" TV mom would exclaim.

"How's my little princess?" Handsome TV dad would call.

"Just fine, Daddy! I'm glad you're finally home!" Darby smiled as she licked the cream off her hands.

"Oh, looks like you've started dinner already! I'm glad that you are eating, sweety. I don't want you to sit here and starve!" TV dad would smile as he would take off his coat and hang it in the foyer closet.

"When Darby has finished with her pie, I'll set dinner out. It's Darby's favorite tonight," TV mom would say prettily.

"Well, whatever that is," TV dad would smile and hug Darby, "I'm sure that it will be delicious. Right, kitten?"

"Right," Darby said thickly, with graham cracker spraying out as she spoke.

The pie tin sat empty on her lap. All gone. Done. Darby opened her eyes wide and looked at the dumpster in front of her. A fly buzzed lazily around a piece of moldering Twinkie that sat near her shoe.

Her legs were dry, but her underwear and socks and shoes were still soaked. She smelled sour and briny. Her stomach felt relieved to know that it wouldn't have to endure school that day. She got up and tossed the pie tin in the dumpster. She looked back at the Twinkie but decided that it probably had germs. She swiped her hand over her face and then tasted the cream and graham cracker crumbs on her fingers. The taste was salty sweet from her tears.

Dirt and grass stuck to the backs of her legs. She tried to brush them away, but they stuck to the cream on her hands.

All she felt was the wetness of her lower body and the stuffed feeling of her belly. It wasn't a bad feeling, except for the swampiness of her Keds.

Darby decided that she had better go home now. Daddy was across town, living with Becky, who used to babysit for Darby when she was little. Darby didn't have to worry about him yelling at her for not going to school or for peeing, because she hadn't seen him since she was four, although he apparently talked with her mother a lot. Her mother was always telling her "Your father is very upset with you about your weight" or "Your father wants you to try this new diet" or "Your father says that you should not be such an awful child." Darby always wondered if her mother really did talk to Daddy, though, because he always had the same things to say that her mother did.

Her mother would still be sleeping from being out so late the night before. Darby didn't know how late she had been out but remembered that she had woken up when the clock said 3:30 a.m. because of a scary dream, and there was no one there. Stumbling into the dark living room, she found a note from the babysitter saying that she had to go home and couldn't wait for Darby's mom any longer. Darby knew that her mother always told the babysitters to just leave at midnight if she was "running late" and she'd pay them later. Her mother ran late a lot.

Now, Darby would go home and wash her uniform in the washing machine. Then she'd take a bath and put her pajamas on and go into her bedroom. She would take the phone book with her and run her finger over her father's name, which was already smeared with her finger's oil. If she didn't accidentally wake her mother up, then maybe her mother would wake up later in a good mood and wouldn't yell at her. Then Darby would just tell her mom that she didn't feel good and had wanted to stay home. But if her mother woke up angry, with headaches and dark mascara streaks under her eyes, Darby didn't know what she'd do. Probably just stay in her room and hope that her mom didn't notice that she was home, which could happen, depending on just how late she had been out and whether or not she had brought home a guest the night before.

But she deserved it if her mother was mad at her. She spent the barrette money on a stupid frozen pie. She was too stupid to even stay on the diet her mother put her on. Her mommy would love her if she were smaller. Her daddy would visit her if she were smaller. She couldn't even control her number one and had gone in her underpants like a baby. If her mother found out, she'd make her wear diapers, even to school. She was bad. She was a bad girl. She deserved all the punishment that she got, even the worst thing her mother could think of, even worse than the time her mother made her eat lard out of the can when she caught Darby eating candy. Her mother was right. Darby was stupid and bad. She was an embarrassment to them all.

She began to walk home, stepping over the cracks in the sidewalk, trying not to let her legs touch so she wouldn't be reminded of what she had done.

"Flarby," she whispered, to no one in particular.

SEVEN MINUTES IN HEAVEN

CLEMENTINE HAD NEVER BEEN KISSED. NOT BEHIND THE BLEACHERS, NOT in the back row of the Megaplex. When Miss H. Catie Wyvern held a press conference at the Royal Observatory in Greenwich, England, and announced that she'd be holding a weekly drawing and each winner would receive one wish granted, whatever they wanted, of course no one believed her, especially when she laid out the requirements: To earn a ticket, all one had to do was initiate a first kiss. It had to be a real kiss, she warned, not a peck on the cheek. You had to feel it.

Two reporters in the front row of the conference, longtime coworkers, each married, turned to the other with eyebrows raised. Then one leaned over and kissed the other, the kiss lasting approximately five seconds. As soon as their lips parted, a soft ping sounded from the ceiling and down floated a bright green ticket that shimmered like lizard skin; it was damp, slightly sticky, and more than a little warm to the touch. The paper—no, it wasn't paper exactly, but something like paper—felt impossibly thin between one's fingers, and it bore the name of the kisser written in a blackish red ink on the back.

"The ticket belongs to the kisser, not the kissed! The drawing is every Tuesday at 3:17 p.m.!" And with that, she stepped off the dais and disappeared into the crowd.

❊   ❊   ❊

First kisses happen every minute, every second of the day, all around the world. During the first week of the contest, people used the drawing as an excuse to kiss pretty strangers or allow them to kiss you. Usually, the better looking of the pair got to initiate and received their name emblazoned on the tiny emerald ticket.

Clementine spent that first week walking down the street with a wry displeasure. It would be her luck, her great misfortune, to have her first kiss be initiated by such a silly, superstitious gimmick! Kissing for prizes! A kiss in exchange for a little green folly.

As it turned out, Clementine was not kissed that first day. She was also not kissed on the second day. In fact, she managed to make it the entire week by simply pretending not to hear the customers at the coffee shop where she worked when they, after ordering their coffee, frequently tacked on "and a kiss" to their order.

On that Tuesday, at precisely 3:17 p.m. in the Royal Observatory in Greenwich, Miss Wyvern announced the name of the winner during another press conference. The winner's true heart's desire was to receive seven trillion dollars. Miss Wyvern rolled her eyes as she announced the wish, with the wisher's identity protected, but then suddenly, an oligarch, who just last week was rumored to be on the brink of bankruptcy, was in the headlines for buying up real estate around Central Park, landing his private jet on Strawberry Fields.

That's when the kissing got urgent.

The next week, Clementine's kiss virginity was endangered at every turn. While walking home or riding the subway, she began turning sideways whenever an eager pair of eyes would scan the crowd. She would pretend to look deeply interested in a text message while tickets appeared and fell around her on all sides, virescent confetti. Would-be kissers hardly waited for permission, although rumors went out that authorities would charge unwanted-kiss perpetrators with sexual assault, tickets or not.

In her little studio apartment next to the highway on-ramp, she tried kissing her cat Lady Macbeth on the mouth, but no ticket appeared. She rubbed tuna water on her mouth until Lady Macbeth licked her lips—no sizzle, no slick little entry popped into being. She kissed the television when her favorite celebrity judged a food competition, the camera close to their mouth, savoring a particularly unctuous morsel. No entry. This was not a real kiss, Clementine knew in her heart, but she just wanted to be certain.

Clementine opted to work the drive-through at the coffee shop, where an opportunity to be smooched unexpectedly was less likely. Although she had offers, certainly. "I have a cold sore," she would murmur. "Leprosy," she said once, but then got a stern talking-to from her manager, a stiff woman with the unlikely name of Mitzy, who then offered to kiss Clementine in front of the staff to prove that Clementine did not have a communicable disease. "No, I would rather not," Clementine demurred.

There were too many people playing this game. In the Royal Observatory, there were now swimming pool-sized plexiglass tanks packed with green lottery tickets, glittering like dragon scales. And this Wyvern woman on the television gave Clementine the shudders. Something was off-putting about her fingers, the long way she reached for the winning ticket, plucking at it the way a mosquito inserts its stylets into the skin to draw blood.

The following week, the next winner was selected: a Gulf War veteran who had lost his legs during a dance across live munitions lurking in the sand and was left with only two puckered thighs. His heart's desire grew back right there on live television, first five tiny nubs popped up on either stump, then toenails grew, followed by a heel, the flesh stretching and lengthening. Viewer discretion was advised. The cameras quickly cut away to the news anchor, an aging but still pretty woman, who was caught kissing the makeup man. A jade paper fluttered down with her name scrawled on the back in shiny letters, still wet and feverish to the touch.

Clementine laid low the following week, wearing a doctor's mask over her mouth. Even with the mask, two men and three women had grabbed her for a fast buss. New pairings were harder to find. Participants carried notebooks. Some played rock-paper-scissors with strangers for quick rasps of lips that lasted just long enough for the familiar ping of the ticket appearing above their heads. Others just took the 50 percent chance of getting an entry with their name on it. She found herself folding her lips into her mouth to and from work just in case.

Why was she being so particular? It was just a kiss. Just a kiss, she thought again, as though such a thing couldn't wake a sleeping princess or befoul an enchantment. The happy ending to every story was punctuated with a first kiss. Her ending, still yet to make itself known, an enchantment that still wanted breaking. Even though on the surface, it seemed like not a big deal, this kiss. And yet. Clementine looked around her studio, the same bare walls she swore she would decorate eight years ago, a single mug on the mug hooks, a stack of overdue library books needing to be returned and the sense of an unspoken voice saying, "Don't forget your library books, honey!" when she leaves for the coffee shop. If only Lady Macbeth knew how to form sentences. Maybe that would be her heart's desire, if she had a ticket, if she were the winner.

The next Tuesday, a young girl, not more than seven years old, won the drawing. Miss Wyvern announced that the child had been emancipated from her birth family, had been adopted by a former First Lady, and the child's biological parents were investigated for child endangerment and abuse. "The heart's desire," Miss Wyvern mentioned, "may be unspoken but can still be the wish granted." She added, "My boss often considers the entirety of the winner's predicament." This was a surprise to everyone, as they had not considered that the wish could be unspoken. The journalists in the room surged forward, microphones in hand.

"Catie! Catie! What is the chemical makeup of the tickets?"

"Wyvern! How does the lottery winner's wish become communicated?"

"Catie! Who is paying for all of this? Is it the United Nations? Is it the Queen? Who is your boss?"

"Ms. Wyvern! Over here. What's your reaction to the *Times* story questioning your identity? Do you have a driver's license or any form of government-issued ID to dispel those rumors? At least tell us what country you're from?"

As ever, she refused to answer any questions. She turned and said, "I prefer Miss Wyvern, not Ms." And then she just stepped out of the lottery showroom and seemed to vanish the moment she exited out of sight.

The reporters refused to leave the room and sat down. In the giant tanks, the tickets began to smolder with dark green smoke that smelled like a mix of rotting cabbages and dead mice. It cleared the room almost instantly and none of the reporters or camera crew were interested in returning.

This new facet of the game intrigued Clementine: If the heart's true desire was revenge, then the wish could be used to dole punishment to the deserving. How interesting. She thought about her attacker, the one whom she never allowed herself to think about, the one who had seemed so kind, had tricked her into going along with him. When it was clear how things were going to go that fateful day, before she sank down into herself, to protect her Clementine-ness from his fists, her last thought was that he would be her first kiss, her first everything.

It turned out he never kissed her, probably unwilling to risk more transfer of DNA. The police said she had been lucky not to lose her eye, lucky that she wasn't pregnant or worse, lucky that she played dead. That's the way they put it, *lucky*, and then asked what she had been wearing, what she had been drinking, what was his name. A sweater (torn and bloody). An apple juice (in a box with a straw, an important detail for a trial that never happened, for a defendant that the detectives had never managed to detect). Marcus Snogglestein (when he had told her his name she had laughed, and he had returned a smirk that should have been her first warning).

Lucky.

It had been the beginning of an enchantment just the same. Since then, she had been safe, but on some level, still asleep, still frozen, still crystalized and unmoving. To would-be kissers, she was pristine; inside, she was damaged.

For the first time in a very long time, Clementine saw something she wanted. Something she could obtain now that she couldn't before. She never knew his real name and the detectives hadn't been able to find him. Not enough evidence, they said, as though she weren't standing right there, evidence of him and everything he did. But Wyvern would find him. Wyvern could draw a Clementine ticket and fulfill Clementine's heart's desire. Clementine's nemesis would know what it was like to escape into his own mind, to try to play dead, to wish that he were actually dead. Most of all, he would know and feel Clementine for the rest of his days. Wyvern would see the necessity of this wish because Clementine was lucky. Her first kiss then would also be the first bit of hope since it happened. A tiny green slip of paper with her name written on it in ink that was theorized to perhaps be blood. *Clementine. Clementine.* She would kiss and kiss and kiss until those kisses set her free.

CAR PEOPLE

I SLIPPED MY HANDS OUT OF MY GLOVES AND INTO MY POCKETS SO THEY'D be warm but not sweaty when I shook her hand. She was standing next to a silver Mercedes-Benz E55, one of the more expensive cars on the lot. It was a lease return that Carleton the Second had picked up from an auction in Florida back when I was still working in the Parts Department. Half the sales team was certain it was never going to sell in Iowa. Half the sales team was certain I would never manage to sell a car, period.

"Hiya there!" I said to her back as she peered into the car windows. Her backpack purse sliding off her shoulder, she jumped backward.

She was beautiful, the sort of sad, delicate beauty of girls who spend too much time in libraries, breathing in dust and not getting enough sun. Blonde hair, the color of corn silk, was tucked neatly behind her ears, which held earrings that seemed too big to be real diamonds. Her clothes were nice but not flashy, luxurious—made of thick fabrics that looked soft, fitting well, not too large or hemmed too short—so the earrings were probably real. Her white fleece hat had ears, like a kitty cat.

Her eyes knocked me off my sales pitch, though. Once I remember hearing Diego talk about the water off Puerto Rico and how just staring out at the ocean would hypnotize him and make him excited to live and at the same time feel like sinking down into it until he drowned on the sandy bottom. And that's the way I felt right then, as though I could have stood there looking forever.

"Hi!" An immediate smile.

"I'm Bobby."

"Hi, Bobby. I'm Katie."

"Hi, Katie."

"Hi."

We both stood there, her watching me with those enormous blue eyes, me rocking on my heels. Then I remembered that the salesman was supposed to be in charge.

"Looks like snow, huh?" I pulled my zipper up higher against the unusually cold October wind.

She looked at the gray ceiling of clouds and shrugged. Her mouth squinched in a cute way, like little kids on juice commercials.

"Hmmm. Maybe?" She smiled again, like she thought that maybe I wanted to hear that answer. I didn't, though. Car salesmen hate snow days; they are customer repellent. The buyers don't want to be freezing their tuchuses off while car shopping, and the sales staff is stuck outside with wet gloves and chapped wrists, knocking snow off, then sweeping the blacktop so the customers won't have to tromp through a drift to check out the latest Jaguar.

"So, can I help you find anything?"

"Um, well, I like this." Her face reflected back at me in the tinted glass of the Benz.

"Nice car. You have excellent taste."

The corners of her mouth curled a little. "It's not my taste really. My grandmother . . . my grandmother used to have one just like this one."

"Grandma has good taste then."

She flicked her eyelashes and twitched. "Had."

"Oh. Sorry to hear that." The wind blew through my coat. I should have brought something warmer.

"Well, I loved it too," she added. "When I was a little girl, she used to pick me up from boarding school on Fridays and drive me home with the sunroof open. And I'd usually be so tired that I'd crash out in the backseat and have these incredible dreams. And then the car would pull up to a stop at the gate, it would wake me up, and everything that sucked from the previous week would just seem silly."

I didn't know what to say to that. Normally customers were pretty guarded when they came onto the lot, so instead I just watched her for a clue. Her gaze drifted to the pinpoint where the road met the horizon beyond the cornfields, and in that moment, there was something in her face, something frail and ghostly hiding there, just beyond my reach.

Her lips parted and she inhaled quickly, as though she were about to say something, but she just sighed, squinted, and shrugged. My hand wanted to touch her, wanted to light upon her shoulder, and maybe graze her cheek. For a moment, she was a lost girl in a department store, the curling photo on a gas station poster, the waxy face staring off a milk carton, but she found herself again, quickly, and she was every girl who ever shot down a guy looking to rock against them during the slow song at a high school dance. My hand decided that it was best to just stay in its pocket.

The loudspeaker spanked the cold air. "Bobby to the tower, please."

"I'll be right back, okay?"

She nodded and looked back at her reflection in the dark windows of the Mercedes-Benz, smoothing her hair as though we were still talking about the weather.

I turned and trotted back to the tower, which was what we called the managers' offices. They were on the second story and had windows that looked down onto the car lot. All deals had to be finalized by either the lot owner, Mr. Rivers, or his son, Carleton the Second. On busy days, a regular staccato of salesman feet on those stairs echoed through the showroom.

*   *   *

Two months ago, I'd been woken up by heavy pounding on my apartment door. Often drunks from the tavern downstairs get lost trying to find the bathroom, but it was the bartender, asking me to throw on my coat and shoes. I followed him, where he pointed at Mr. Rivers, the owner of the car lot I worked at, sitting in the corner, sobbing into his whiskey and water, a dark stain at his crotch. I got Mr. Rivers cleaned up, gave him a dry pair of gray sweatpants, hoisted him into my ancient pickup truck, and drove him back to his house. On Monday morning, I was summoned from the Parts Department to the tower.

My friends in Parts had shaken their heads when they heard that I'd be joining the big boys out on the pavement. Gus, the parts manager, put his hand on my shoulder and sighed. "Bobby, there are people people and then there are car people. You and me, we're car people, Bobby."

The general feeling in Parts was that the sales crew was a bunch of pricks and assholes. That was the punch line to this great joke that Zubby in the detailing shop told me once, but damned if I can remember how it went. Something about a proctologist, I think. I'm bad at remembering jokes. But every good salesman should know some jokes, so I memorized three clean ones from *Reader's Digest* to tell to customers during any awkward pauses. One is about a grasshopper going into a bar, one about the Chicago Bears, and the third about a guy playing golf. I keep trying to learn more, but it seems like my brain can only hold onto three at a time. I figure that most people don't buy more than one car a year, so that works out just fine.

*   *   *

When I got up to the tower, Carleton the Second was leaning back in his chair, languidly toying with his mouse over a mouse pad that showed a muskie jumping. He had suitcases on the visitors' chairs, so I decided to stand. I could see the reflection of a solitaire game in the windows behind him.

"Bobby? I just need to talk with you for a quick minute before I'm out of here." His eyes never left the screen.

"Sure can! For as many minutes as you want!" I grinned a little, but Carleton the Second didn't smile back, so I stopped.

"I saw that you showed the '97 Passat to Rick Davis the other day. How did that go?"

I broke out in a big smile. "Oh, it went great! It was a graduation present for his daughter, and I think she's going to like it."

"Well, I was watching and I noticed you took him right over to the older imports."

I nodded warily, starting to feel like this was a test. "He said he wanted a used car, something that was young feeling for his daughter but also safe and low payments. And that wasn't brown."

"Okay, okay, but you walked him right past a Miata and the Saab 9S. The feel of the wheel will seal the deal, right? It shouldn't have been anything less than a 20K sale."

It was bugging me the way that Carleton the Second was acting like he was Mr. Davis's best drinking buddy. "He specifically said he wanted something moderately priced for his daughter. And he was really happy, too!"

"Yeah, I'll bet he was. You talked him into saving ten grand." He finally looked up from the computer. "I know you don't know everyone in town like the other guys, Bobby, but there are things you can watch out for. He drove onto the lot in a Lexus. He was wearing an expensive watch. That means you can push him to a high-end model and that means a bigger voucher for you. I know this was your first sale, so it's no big deal—it's just something to think about in the future. You're not making your nut right now. You know, we've talked about this. Commissions. You need to make enough in commissions to justify your draw. But right now, you're behind. You're not making your draw. So, be strong, okay, Bobby? If you're not strong, you're what?" He waited for me to answer, fidgeting with the computer mouse.

"Weak." I replied, finishing one of the repeated catchphrases from our Monday morning sales meetings. Carleton the Second always liked to say things like "goal building" and "The coffee is only for closers" and management crap like "growing our business," which was dumb because he wasn't going to let us forget that it was his business and not ours. I wanted to say something about how it wasn't right to force someone to spend more than they wanted to just because they make more money, but I already knew that wasn't a winning paradigm, or whatever it was that they called it. That kind of thinking was weak, not strong. And I already knew I wasn't the kind of strong that Carleton the Second liked to see. I had problems remembering most of the rhymes they tried to teach us. Things like that just seemed to be there and try as I might, I remember and then I don't.

"Atta boy! Good luck today! Make lots of money!" He made guns with his hands and pretended to shoot me, then turned back to the monitor as though he had just given me the best gift ever. I turned and walked back out into the main office. From the windows, I could see Katie pacing outside. Crap. I had forgotten a whole girl outside.

I had been happy in the Parts Department, but now I was out on the lot, and I knew that was a step up. And I loved smelling that mixture of WD-40, Turtle Wax, and wet pavement while the little triangular plastic flags snapped at me from above. Even on a day like today, when Carleton the Second made me feel like I wasn't worth the sales time. Selling was easier than parts, at least it had less numbers. Then there were people like Katie. She had just told me that her family had money. Little things I was supposed to pay attention to. Close the deal. I could remember that.

I trotted back out to her on the lot—you gotta hustle and always be running when the customer sees you. I got ready to make my clincher, the grappling hook that seals the deal, Carleton the Second called it. Something like "There's another couple who have an appointment to come see this beauty, she won't last long" or "You don't see deals like that in Iowa, huh?" but I didn't get a chance to because she cleared her throat and said, "Okay, let's do this."

"Want to take it for a demo?" I exclaimed, a little too loudly. "I mean, we don't usually let people joyride in cars over uh, a certain range of luxury, but if you're serious, I can take your driver's license and let you take it out."

"Yeah. Let's do it. My father says that he'll buy me whatever car I want. And, um—this one is nice."

Her face went blank and her voice was completely dead when she mentioned her dad. Her dad, the son of the lady with the Benz? Could have been. Close the deal, Bobby. Make your nut for once. But it felt like I was missing something in the conversation again, something another salesman would have caught right away. I must have looked uncertain because she smiled in a way that reminded me of school pictures, her mouth in a half circle but her eyes staying the same. She handed me the license and I snapped a photo of it quick with my phone. My screen was cracked and the slash went across her photo, but the actual file would be okay. Her smile on the license felt real in a way that her smile in person didn't.

"Okay, let me get the keys to open the box and then you can take her out." I spun on my heels and trotted back into the building.

We're supposed to go on test drives with anyone under thirty and any customer who comes in by themselves, but it felt unfriendly. I reached out, letting the key ring dangle off an extended pinky finger. Why my pinky finger? I didn't know. She responded by extending her pinky finger, brushing mine as she lifted the keys.

"Perfect," she said softly.

I walked into the showroom, past the new models and end-of-year closeouts, into the huddle of gray modular particleboard salesmen desks. On my desk, I found a little box with a fancy silver key chain in it, complete with the REA logo. There was also a handwritten note from Mr. Rivers, congratulating me on my first sale. I looked across the sales floor to his glass office, where he was reading his plane tickets to someone on the phone. He was semi-retired and mostly only came in on Fridays to sign our paychecks, but today, he and his son were leaving for a GMAC convention in Las Vegas. I liked Mr. Rivers, not just because he gave me the promotion that changed my life, but also because he always acted like he was interested in what I had to say. I decided that I wouldn't use the key chain because I'd just scratch it on something or bend it or drop it down a storm drain. I'd keep it for good, keep it safe somewhere. But I would thank him for it when he had a moment. That's the kind of guy he was.

When Mr. Rivers wasn't in, Carleton the Second walked around like he was the boss. In my opinion, he's not my boss until a "II" appears in the name on the dotted line of my paycheck. I accidentally called him Junior back when I first started. I had heard a bunch of the guys in the garage call him Chuck Junior and assumed that was what he preferred until everyone heard me and started laughing behind coughs. Carleton the Second had pretended not to notice me for a long time after that. If it had been up to him, I'm pretty sure I would still be spending fifteen minutes every night trying to scrub the grease out from the cracks in my fingers.

* * *

Most test drives last about twenty minutes. Three and a half hours later, Katie and the Benz hadn't come back. It was almost five o'clock and the lot was about to close.

"You didn't even get a copy of her driver's license! You don't even know her last name!" Ira's face was red and he spat a bit on my REA jacket as he yelled. I don't know why I lied to him about it. I guess I knew the Benz would turn up again, once Katie had her fun. No reason to get her into trouble when I was going to get screamed at no matter what. And Ira really shouldn't have been mad about the copy of the license. We were a small-town dealership and rarely took a photocopy of a driver's license. Mr. Rivers thought it seemed unfriendly, but Ira was just looking for more things to scream about, so I didn't bring that up, just let him holler.

"We ought to call the police, but we're not going to. Not tonight. Junior's going to be back from Vegas day after tomorrow. The only way you're going to save your job, green pea or not, is if that car ends up back here without a scratch before he does. We can keep it our little secret, but you better hope it's a drive and ditch." Ira stormed out the glass double doors of the show floor toward his ivory Town Car.

"Don't worry about it, Bobby. It happens to all of us," Cheri said softly behind me.

"Has it happened to you?"

"Well, no." I heard her take a breath as though to say something else and then let it escape slowly.

"Yeah, that's what I thought."

"We're just lucky Junior isn't here, right? At least it's Ira and he's not calling Rivers right now."

"Well, it doesn't look too good for him that it happened on his watch, now does it?"

"But he's right. It's probably a drive and ditch. It's that time of year, you know. Halloween is next week, and the kids are pledging fraternities and sororities, that kind of thing."

I didn't say anything back because I didn't trust myself to talk around the meatball stuck in my throat, so Cheri just kept going.

"You ever notice there are no church bells in the entire county? Because every fall, they get thrown over a bridge into the Iowa River. It's a prank. They'll go for a joyride and then leave it somewhere. Either that or the car might turn up in the lot sometime in the middle of the night. You know, like they wait for everyone to leave and then return it. Big joke, har har, it's all just so they have something to tell their grandchildren. You'll see, sweetie. It will be okay."

"Carleton the Second is going to shit a bird. Absolutely shit a bird." I didn't like to swear. My mom always told me that it was a sign of poor upbringing, but this seemed like a good time to do it and it made me feel an ounce better about lying about the license.

"It will be okay," she repeated, but I don't think even she believed it. I walked out to the employee parking lot and climbed into my truck so I wouldn't have to say anything else to anyone.

I took the long way home, between fields of finished sunflowers and walls of dried corn stalks. A light snow had begun to fall at some point, but I didn't notice it until I needed my windshield wipers. There were gray battleship-shaped clouds threatening to cover up the weak ball of sun. The back of my throat burned like rusty metal and battery acid. A stolen car! And it was my fault. There would be police in the morning. They might even think I was in on it. It was all so bad. I was in trouble, no bones about it.

I thought about the Parts Department, about Gus saying that we were car people and not people people. And that's the thing about cars, once you understood them, you knew what made them run and what made them stop. And you could count on that. People, you just never could trust what you knew about them. I thought about the night as it stretched out ahead of me. I'd get home, heat up a Hungry-Man dinner, peel back the foil to expose the tater tots, and sit with a Miller High Life watching television. And I thought about how they'd probably make me clean the snow off the cars in the morning before they fired me.

And that's when I saw the Benz.

The shape was unmistakable, a stylized curve of platinum that had no rightful business among the pale stalks of corn. When I got closer, I could see the windows were all down. At first, I worried that they were busted out, but that just seemed silly, thinking about a girl smashing out the windows. Unless she had been a decoy and had given the car to someone else. A boyfriend maybe. I could see my dealer plate on the back with "Bobby" neatly written in Sharpie above the number. It just about broke my heart.

I parked my truck next to the car. It was a drive and ditch, like Ira had said, and maybe the keys would be somewhere nearby. In fact, if I was real lucky, I could walk the cornfield and find them glittering within the tractor ruts before nightfall and return the car and it would be there in the morning to show Ira. I knew that she hadn't meant any harm. Maybe she hadn't thrown them too far. I decided that she had been alone. It was a dare, maybe for a sorority. There couldn't be a boyfriend. No. Not Katie.

I hopped out of the truck and groaned when I saw that the sunroof was open too. How long had it been sitting here like this? Had the snow fallen into a cold or a warm car? If the leather seats were ruined, it was just as bad as a stolen car as far as Carleton the Second was concerned. I stuck my head in the window and exhaled when I saw the keys dangling from the ignition like a lady's earrings. I almost started crying with gratitude.

On the front seat was Katie's white kitty cat hat and her backpack purse, open. And a medicine bottle and a can of diet soda and a puff of wadded Kleenex. And that's when I noticed that Katie was in the backseat.

She was laying there, hands folded under her cheek, looking for all the world like a doll. I hung half in and out of the window, my fingers grasping the door and snow making icy prickles where my shirt had ridden up. I held my breath, waiting for her chest to rise and fall, rise and fall, rise and fall, because she must have been only napping there on those fine leather seats, had to be only napping. And when my lungs caught on fire, I took another gasp and held my breath again, counting to sixty-seven in my head until my ears pounded. Then I exhaled.

She never moved.

No little sighs, no soft exhales, no goose bumps making the fine blonde hairs of her arm stand up. Nothing. Snowflakes dusted her cheeks like tiny freckles and all I could think was that they should have been melted, but they weren't. They should have melted. She wasn't napping. Maybe it had started out that way, but it wasn't a nap anymore. I had wanted to grab her right then, fold my arms around her, and hold her while six car salesmen watched from a hundred feet away. I wanted to do that badly. And I didn't.

Somewhere in the distance, a train whistled in the thin light and nudged me back into action. I reached in through the window and opened the door softly, like I was worried about waking her up. A quick turn of the keys and the good old German engine came to life with a throaty growl. I clicked the car into reverse and pulled out slowly, feeling the stalks of corn brush against the undercarriage.

I put it into drive and eased off the gravel onto the long gray ribbon of road before us. The sunflower field looked like a choir of children, bowing their heads as I drove Katie past them.

The railroad tracks ran parallel to the highway out of town. The whistle blasted a low dirge into the crisp air and my face froze in the wind from the open sunroof and then we were nose and nose with the engine of the train, racing along at 45, 50, 55 and climbing. The sun was sinking down behind the skeletal black trees, turning all of the frost into magic and the train was blowing, clearing our path, and I was thinking the Benz and me and Katie, we could just drive like this forever.

INTERSOMNOLENCE

ELLE IS MAKING LISTS. THINGS TO DO BEFORE SHE DIES (LATEST ENTRY: walk confidently in high heels). Things that she needs to spend money on (renew car registration, yogurt, tampons). Words that sound funny after you say them repeatedly (e.g., tampons, smorgasbord, glean) and what they start to sound like (glean = the word for fornication in the language of Sleestacks). The people who contribute the quotes on the sides of her Starbucks cups (Most recent: Mitch Hedberg). The wonderful things homeless people have said to her ("Thank you for being alive." "You are beautiful. No, I mean it. Gorgeous.") and the wonderful things they have said that were not said directly to her ("I don't need a gun. I got Jesus. Shoot THAT, motherfucker!") Places she wants to visit (Latest entry: the Maldives to swim with giant jellyfish). The number of times that Jasper, her fellow polysomnograph coworker, says that X is "better than hot buttered sex" (#42 as of 12:30 a.m. during last shift, where X = a 1972 Camaro).

She maintains two separate lists this evening: Reasons Why I
Might Die and My Ideal Jeopardy Categories. Each item is written
with a neat little bullet point that embosses the page:

- I, at this moment, do not have enough gas in my car to escape
  attacks from terrorists, aliens, zombies, etc.

- Cell phone battery dead (see above re: zombies, terrorists, et al.)

- I do not like dark green vegetables (antioxidants, vitamins, free
  radicals, etc.)

- The Film Oeuvre of Sofia Coppola

- Road Signs as Seen from the Backseat of a Vista Cruiser in the '70s

There are forty-eight places in the human head that require electrodes. She can sing them off in her sleep. Not sleep. Elle doesn't
talk in her sleep. This she knows, because she's watched a video
of her sleeping-self. There can be no doubt that she dreams. As
with all things, there is scientific proof in the form of polysomnogram. It's impossible for the normal human brain to not dream. Elle
dreams but simply does not remember. She knows this for a fact.
Working graveyard as a polysomnography technician at the sleep
lab, she has the luxury of complimentary brain scans and she has
seen proof that her parietal lobe is pristine and undamaged, a plum
of an organ, so much better than, say, her liver. She has held her
dreams in her hand on a black-and-white printout. They look like
bunny tracks in the snow. Elle imagines her dream bunnies hiding
behind her conscious mind and wonders if they get together during
the day to talk shit about her. She senses them gathering at the edg-
es of her peripheral vision, sparkles along the corners of her eyes
like the symptom of retinal detachment. Silly rabbits.

Before there were electric lights, the Victorians slept an average of nine to ten hours a night, adjusting for the changes of the

seasons accordingly. Researchers know this from diaries, although Elle wonders what the Victorians might have thought of their sleep disorders. Humours would need to be drained, uteruses palpated, perhaps they would employ the use of magnets to realign the senses. If she lived in the time of bustles and pessaries, Elle suspects that doctors would have thought she had a demon sitting on her chest at night, stealing her breath, or perhaps simply an acute case of the vapors.

- Victorian Birth Control
- Brain damage
- Brain tumor
- Brain weevil
- That thing in *Star Trek* that goes into your ear and fucks up your personality
- Alien Life Forms from *Star Trek: The Original Series*

Before entering the stage of rapid eye movement, the average sleeper moves around a lot. This is when sleepwalking and sleep talking happens, but then, there's a moment of silence that is a precursor to dreaming. You can watch from closed-circuit cameras, and you don't even need to look at the machines to know that their muscle tension has gone slack, their chin droops forward like a ventriloquist dummy's waiting for a line. If they're not already hooked up to a CPAP mask, they start to snore, and then *blam*, the delta indicators start making wavy lines, curving into a twisted mountain road pattern, the topographical map of the Oregon Trail.

She hopes for a day when the machines will spit out dreams as actual pictures instead of images of electric currents. Right now, they only have gray matter seismic activity. In the morning over breakfast bars and bowls of corn flakes, the subjects must write in journals about their night, describing their dreams in detail. Some are vivid, with plots and subplots, supporting casts and Vonnegut-esque prose. Elle compares these to the electro-encephalograph for each sleeper. No aliens. No loves lost or hard fought. No fortune cookie slips. Just static on an unused television channel. A dream about Milton Berle and the first pet you've ever owned making sweet, sweet love (hot buttered sex) out on top of the Eiffel Tower while you float beside them playing Jenga is a Category 8 earthquake that could level San Francisco.

Elle tries not to think about the dreams when she sees them on paper. She tries not to think about what, focusing instead on the simple question of are they or aren't they dreaming? She thinks about the patients who smell like stale cigarettes or dirty laundry in the morning from their nocturnal hyperhydration or the occasional bed wetter or masturbatory emission (which is why all of the mattresses are coated in plastic, like at summer camp. Sometimes if the subject is a stomach sleeper, the lab techs get an adrenaline rush, thinking that someone is choking, and rush into the pods, expecting to save a life only to discover that it's just the snore microphone picking up the crinkle of the piss plastic.)

The lab observation room smells like ozone and static. Jasper pulls the label off a bottle of water and checks his text messages. The other technician, Humza, buzzes in the first patient, and they watch the top of her head enter the elevator.

- Too much caffeine!!!
- Fashion Trends of the 1980s

Tonight, Jasper is taking sleep pods 1 and 2, Humza is taking 3, 4, and 5, and Elle is taking 6 and 7. Humza finds the sensation of parting the hairs of strangers to be very disturbing, so Elle measures the heads of his subjects as well as her own, and he brings her a soy chai tea latte every night. It's a good relationship. Sometimes when they have a very elderly subject, Humza saves Elle from the horror of yellowed old man toenails. If one of them uses the word "Saturday" while wiring, this is code for "Insane Amounts of Body Odor, Please Kill Me Now" or "This Old Dude Just Tried to Grab My Ass" and usually someone will come in to help. Why is it always the geezers who pinch asses? It is a mystery that Elle enjoys contemplating. She is also amused by the thought that any resulting litigation would require a lawyer to use the term "morning wood" and that it will be dutifully transcribed on a long tape by someone who probably hates their life more than Elle does.

In her lab coat, worn only for show, Elle fades in and out of focus. The white coat lends a level of authority to the electrodes and smelly glue that they plop merrily onto skulls, knowing that the dried glue will come off in chunks with hair still attached, looking for all the world like a case of leprosy or perhaps syphilis.

Room 5 already contains Humza's first subject, waiting in a Proenza Schouler T-shirt and pristine yoga pants. Five is a forty-three-year-old socialite whose snoring is an embarrassment during ski weekends. Elle quickly circumnavigates this woman's cranial landscape with a tape measure and grease pencil, dotting her head with Os to mark each electrode site. After Five, she moves onto Six, then Three, then Four. She sings, to the Slinky commercial jingle, her wire song to herself as she glues (Oh Chin EMG, Central EEG, Occipital EEG, EKG oh my oximeter and thermistor and EOG and leg EMG and OMG WTF go to sleep you!), air compressor in hand, blowing the glue fumes away from herself and the subject. She'll be slightly high for at least twenty minutes after the fifth head. She mentally bids adieu to four thousand brain cells.

She hears Jasper over the loudspeaker in Room 7 across the hall, telling the subject to get dressed in their pajamas and someone will be in shortly, which means that he must be done with his rooms already and he and Humza are about to begin. Humza's voice through the overhead speaker is an aural caramel macchiato while Jasper's is an espresso—a jolt to the brain, the sensation of teeth vibrating, a sharp intake of breath. Elle is a vanilla Frappuccino, cold and bland. A drink not to be taken seriously. The bits of real vanilla bean are just a constellation of birthmarks, signs that she really needs to do more skin cancer self-checks.

- Malignant Melanoma
- Viral internet videos

Seven is a hypertensive banker with obstructive sleep apnea. His nose is gigantic, and she loses her measuring stride when she has to go digging through the supply closet for the extra-large mask, all the while listening to Enya play over the loudspeaker, the soundtrack to spas, retreats, and sleep laboratories. Maybe also funeral homes, with that "Only Time" song.

When Elle runs the nocturnal myoclonus leg wires, the banker has an erection. She almost makes a comment, for the benefit of Humza and Jasper, that some things don't require an extra-large but then remembers that she is in the room with the banker, not sitting in the lab playing straight man to their Statler and Waldorf.

At her desk, there is an unsigned note from Jasper (identifiable by the way he prints everything, as though his right hand is stuck in seven-point font) tucked into the spine of her open notebook. She wonders briefly if he has read anything she has written but decides that he would not have resisted commenting on her death list. He has noted a few of Six's readings: the time of system checks and the subject's subsequent sleep latency.

- Secondhand smoke from having grown up when people didn't care about smoking around kids

- Driving too fast after work when it is still dark and hitting a deer that will get stuck in my windshield and before I unbuckle the seatbelt to hide in the backseat, the deer kicks me to death

- Potent Potables

Six is already throwing theta waves, indicating that she's in that hazy stage of pre-sleep. Before Elle started working in the sleep lab, she found this stage of sleep delicious, because random thoughts would pop into her head and it was as close to lucid dreaming as she had ever experienced. Now, whenever Elle sees theta waves, she must focus on not unconsciously clenching her own muscles. The slightest movement, the off noise and you jolt awake, causing a minor autonomic adrenaline response. There is the constant worry that her sleeper will be too irritated by the wires glued to their scalp, the nasal airflow monitor feeling foreign and tugging against one cheek or the other. One misstep and the statistical reliability of every reading for the next several hours are called into question as an outlier. Elle hates outliers. Outliers make blips on her final report and for every one, there is an asterisk and a footnote. She prefers her charts to have lovely trending data, graceful slopes upward and down with corresponding respiration and heart rate numbers, an elegant standard deviation on her ANOVAs. An aesthetically pleasing histogram confirms her faith in science, that everything has an answer. Everything.

- Jane Austen

- Nail biting: microscopic tears in gums are entryway for bacteria into the bloodstream, i.e., massive heart infection and subsequent death

- Meals You Only Need to Add Water To
- Myocardial infarction from too many hot dogs

Three is on his back, snoring, his tongue falling back and causing an obstruction. From the exertion of breathing, his neck wattle flutters, rapidly like a fetal beating heart under an ultrasound.

"He's going to need a CPAP sleep mask if he obstructs six more times in the next ten minutes. Note it: 11:43 p.m." Elle resists waking up Three. She'd have to deal with his breath to fit the mask properly. Jasper could never keep his eyes on his own work.

Each subject begins to murmur. Elle slips her shoes back on and faces her bank of monitors. The observation of subjects does funny things in her head and sometimes she will reach to move a strand of hair out of a subject's mouth. She usually manages to stop her hand just before it hits the glass of the monitor, and right now, her fingers itch to fix Six's pajama top that seems to be binding around her neck. Elle loves watching the subject's public face dissolve and their real personality come out, all readable by the graphic nudity of their sleeping faces. The details of the scandals may be ambiguous, but the worried expressions, their hidden shames, all presented on a tousled, billowy canvas. There is a reason that sleep clothes are called intimates. This transition, the ripping away of the public veneer is much more fascinating and exciting to Elle than a person's wrinkled nipple or mushroom-capped penis.

The later it gets, the busier the night, the more she stares at the trails of brainwaves scrolling across her screen, she will fade into the starkness of the plain white walls until she is just a set of blue irises floating in midair. Sometimes when she goes home after a long shift and closes her eyes to fall asleep, she sees the spiking and trailing amperage of thought patterns. The human brain has a lot in common with a kitchen blender. Five hundred years ago, sleep apnea was a succubus, hovering above your prone form, or a fragment of undercooked potato.

- Chapstick and lip emollients
- Slide off a bridge on icy roads, car plunges into the water and cannot open doors due to water pressure, subsequently: drowning
- I decide to put on a pair of shoes I haven't worn in a while and then get bitten by a poisonous spider hanging out in the toe
- Dorothy Parker-isms

At 5:30 a.m., it starts to hail. Elle looks out over the glimmer of dawn, which looks like the inside of a popcorn popper. She wonders if any of the sleepers are dreaming about flying.

Seven's brain is waking up, making beta patterns, his conscious mind winning the fight against lemurs wearing hats who drive Chryslers and his ability to remember the language of flowers.

She unhooks his wires from the network, swings them up over his neck and ties them into a loose bow. He resembles a large, rumpled electric squid. He has another erection. She pointedly avoids making eye contact but can tell that this time, he's embarrassed. She instructs him to use the bathroom and that someone will be back to start detaching him from all the diodes and sensors. She checks in on Six, who is still deep in delta, and passes Humza on his way back from the kitchen with a granola bar and a Styrofoam cup of orange juice with a bendy straw, which means that the lab assistant hasn't arrived yet. Elle smiles, knowing this means the banker will be alone for a while, left to think about what he has done.

Jasper is sitting in the lab playing Minesweeper in a small corner of one of his monitors, constantly craning his head back to the big screen to see if One or Two has started throwing some beta or alpha waves. Humza pokes his head in the door.

"Hey, Sheila just called. She's not coming in today."

"Oh . . . slacker."

"No, some asshat in a pickup T-boned her car. She's fine. Car's totaled, though. But, thought you should know that you can't pawn Mister Happy Pants off on anyone. And he's starting to bitch," Humza grimaces, and in that brief moment, Elle's stomach flutters at the pursing of his lips. "That means we're on sheet duty too!" and his head disappears.

Without the daytime lab assistant, the three must handle all of their end-of-shift duties plus all of the prep work that normally gets done long after they have finished their scoring and gone home, like sanitizing wires, sorting and replacing everything they had used during the night, and stripping and remaking beds. Normally, their subjects are gone by 8 a.m. and then they can devote a few hours to completing the polysomnogram scores, but they spend an hour looking for electrode cups, and then another fifteen minutes trying to find the D-clips (which are used with electrodes but inexplicably not stored anywhere near the electrode cups) and an extra twenty minutes griping about how they should have two lab rats anyway and how royally fucked they are.

- Shot during late-night convenience store robbery gone wrong
- Complications due to overly strained bladder (ex. Tycho Brahe)
- The Oscars

By the time they are done with the tear down and set up, it is almost noon and they have been awake an average of 17.4 hours (Jasper does a quick Excel formula and then mentions that it would have been closer to 19 hours if Humza hadn't basically stumbled out of bed and driven to work, throwing off the average). Humza and Jasper decide to brew some of the lab's coffee (tasting of dirt and melancholy, with just a hint of cat urine), power through their scoring, and take a nap at the lab rather than going home to sleep and then coming back for their next shift.

Elle weaves her way through the day shift workers on their way back from lunch and hates them, just a little bit, for all of their options, so many restaurants that cater just to them. The sun is drilling holes into her cornea and the thought of coming back in a handful of hours to score before the next subjects come in is unbearable.

She manages to make it back to the lab by 6:30 p.m. Humza and Jasper are sleeping in pods right next to each other, 3 and 5. She knows this because she can see them on the video monitors when she walks into the lab. They have left her a note to wake them before 7 p.m. Elle sips her venti triple-shot mocha and watches them sleep, waiting for the caffeine to wiggle its way through her brain and fire up the synapses. Jasper and Humza aren't hooked up to machines, so it's a bit like watching a foreign movie without subtitles. She can't even tell something as basic as whether they are dreaming or not. Jasper sleeps on his back, arms at his side, in what is called the soldier position, a position favored by kings and presidents. Humza is a starfish, arms thrown up on his pillow as though in surrender, his legs sprawled. There is not a single spot on the plastic-covered mattress that could accommodate another person, not even if she curled up tightly against him.

Elle already knows that she sleeps on her side; her own sleep study video from her orientation at the sleep lab confirmed this. Her arms are always outstretched, sometimes as though cupping an invisible fragile object. Maybe in her dreams she is carrying baby birds or engaging in some kind of circus act involving crystal balls or snow globes. Sometimes she wakes up in this position, her fingers are outstretched, the sheets wrinkled, a white cotton Zen garden of neat furrows. Maybe instead of highly structured plotlines, she just organizes and rearranges a very messy pantry during her entire dream cycle, labels all facing outward, and when she awakens, she was just reaching for a box of cereal. Hardly worth remembering.

She opens the case files on Six, queues up the sleep video and plays it in triple fast speed, charting the times and circling notable trends to forward to the subject's sleep specialist. She plots Six's graphs and statistics while playing Seven's sleep video in double time, watching the patterns and listening to him do his somniloquy in a high-pitched Chipmunk voice. Then she pauses, backs up the replay, and listens to it in real time. She goes back to Six's scores and notes the initiation of delta waves, then queues Six's video to 11:58, the same moment as Seven's strange comment, and hits play.

Six says, very clearly, "The girl with the sheets should wear a seatbelt."

Seven's comment almost overlaps with Six's. "Pickup truck does not stop."

She compares their deltas. While Six entered her Phase 3 sleep much earlier than Seven, they both remain in delta for the normal length of time. Elle remembers that the previous night, almost all of the patients were in delta at the same moment. She pulls up One's video. She queues it to 11:58 and pushes play.

"It's a bad intersection."	"There goes her premium."
"The girl with the sheets should wear a seatbelt."	"Hail, hail, the gang's all here."
"Pickup truck does not stop."	"Guy is an asshat."
"Close call for Sheila."	

She sits at the pod, staring into the monitors. There is a moment of restlessness amid the sleepers, and then, at 12:04:

"Japanese school girl fetish."   "Little Star Twins."

"Cat that is not a cat."

"Answer in a question, moron."

"Face that launched a thousand   "What is a Fender guitar, Alex."
malls."

"Frog cat another cat rabbit dog."

Her hand is shaking as she flips up the video surveillance of the sleep lab and at 12:03, she watches herself chew on the edge of her pen, then write in her notebook on the top of a new page. She already knows what is on the page but flips open her notebook to confirm. At the top of the second page of her ideal Jeopardy categories:

- The World of Hello Kitty

The next five minutes are without comment. Then she watches herself write in her notebook. Before her pen leaves the page:

"No spider."   "Martyr girl."

"Painful death."   "Angel."

"No, icy bridge."   "So young. Too   "No stopping it."
                          young."

Her hands are asleep. On the video, Elle and Humza both look at their screens and start typing madly. Six and Three have gone into REM cycle.

"More!" she hisses at the screen, as though trying not to wake up the sleepers. She feels coffee burble in her stomach, so she leans forward in plane crash position, breathing through her mouth and waiting to throw up into the trash can under the desk, but nothing happens. From the video, Four tells someone to get off his foot. Two minutes later, One asks his absent wife if she paid the credit card bill. Seventeen minutes later, he calls someone a "Turd Bugle" and then, as if to prove a point, farts.

Elle forwards through everything at quadruple speed. The seven sleepers cycle in and out of delta, but never all at the same time. Elle replays the time between 11:43 and 12:11 again. She should go wake up Humza and Jasper and show them—whatever this was—play them the tapes and try not to cry when they talk about the girl dying young. She should. She should—something. She looks at the charts again, all perfectly normal and boring when split apart, dissonant, and strange and exceptional when thrown together.

One theory of sleep is that dreams are just a nighttime hallucination that the brain simply strings together into a meaningful narrative, which means that all of the sleep talking Elle hears on the video playback is just a series of words, echolalia from the day tossed together with her own mind making connections. It's like reading a horoscope in the paper. Mercury is in retrograde and the sleepers are air signs.

Humza and Jasper stumble into the lab, groggy and swearing, but stop complaining when they see that she has brought each of them coffee. Elle watches the videos again as she's buzzing in the subjects, taking notes, and then it is 8 p.m., and they are all busy gluing electrodes to the heads of fresh subjects and testing equipment. Tonight, her Six is a football coach with night terrors and her Seven is the insomniac dean of a little private performing arts college with a crazy silver thicket of hair that makes navigating the electrode sites difficult. Elle puts everything out of her mind and focuses on the numbers, the addition and subtraction of measurements, division by two, and then the tight swimmy scent of adhesive filling her head. She says nothing to Humza or Jasper. She is a true scientist, this above all things. She wants to make sure that their bias won't skew tonight's data.

All subjects tucked into bed for the night, Jasper announces lights out and then slumps down, puts his head on his desk and groans. Humza asks if it's okay with them if he streams techno off the internet because he's going to be dead by 10 p.m. if something doesn't wake him up. Elle cracks the tired ache out of her fingers and watches the overhead projection of the seven people each trying to find the cool spot on their pillows. Jasper wonders if they shouldn't make another run for coffee and Humza declares that he's going to use his overtime pay to go to Amsterdam because it gives him something to look forward to instead of feeling sorry for himself. Jasper tells him to go fuck himself.

Elle worries that the insomniac will ruin everything, but she had managed to convince the woman to take a sleeping aid to counteract the discomfort of the wires, and already Seven is heading into light delta, followed by Four, then Two, then Three. Five thrashes a bit, twisting his wires into the pillow, and then Six throws K-complexes and is out. Elle sits absolutely still, eyes flipping from Five to One to Five to One. Five offers up a deep gulping snort that Elle is certain will wake him, but he ekes it out and slumps into delta sleep. Which leaves One.

Elle stares at the overhead, muscles clenched so hard that she realizes her neck is aching from the angle. She shakes it out. Six shouts something about peanut butter. Jasper is flipping through the take-out menus and arguing with Humza about which was the better '70s movie: *Cannonball Run* or *Every Which Way but Loose*. When Jasper makes the argument for Dom DeLuise, One throws her first delta wave.

Elle waits for a second, to see if it will hold, then spins her chair around to her workstation. She queues up all videos and audio at once, hunches down, throws her headphones on to drown out the lab noise, and stares down at the sleeping bodies. Her ears are filled with the slow, even breathing of seven strangers. There seems to be a slight upturning of their mouths, as though they know she is watching, that this time she is listening. She does not breathe and hears the blood pound in her ears, in staccato relief against the exhalations. Finally in a voice she can only hope is a whisper, she breaks.

"Tell me. What happens to me. Please. Just tell me."

She closes her eyes and waits for a response.

BILLET-DOUX

Dear Guy with iPod on the 7:20 p.m. Train in from Berkeley,

Do I know you? Except that I know that I don't, because I don't know anyone in California yet. So you're a mystery to me. One that I will figure out.

Sincerely,

Nancy Drew (aka Liz)

Dear Cubicle Desk,

What the hell is the greasy stuff that you keep getting on my pants? Where is it coming from? Why are you making me feel so inept and stupid? Also, do you think you could be *more* exposed to the world, the way you're positioned so my ass faces back into the department? It's a feng shui nightmare. You're too low, also. It's not ergonomically acceptable.

Regrettably yours,

Liz

Dear Owen Meany,

You've ruined me for all men.

> Keep passing the open windows,
>
> Liz

Dear iPod Guy,

On the ride home, you looked at me and did that eyebrow raise thing that people do when they recognize someone from somewhere. Who do you think I look like, iPod Guy? The girl who sells you your coffee? The fifth clarinet in marching band, the one who couldn't walk and also play Sousa at the same time? Do you wonder what I'd look like with braces and maybe I could be her? Or maybe I'm the girl who used to babysit for you when you were eight? Maybe you just think I'm cute. Maybe. Or I buttoned my shirt wrong again. Tomorrow I'll pass you a note that says

Do you think I'm cute?

CHECK ONE:

( ) YES ( ) NO ( ) MAYBE

> Sincerely,
>
> Liz

PS Kidding!

PPS ( ) YES ( ) NO (X) MAYBE

Dear Crazy People on BART,

You're very unnerving sometimes. The way you carry on conversations with no one and if I listen long enough, they almost start to make sense and become somewhat beautiful, like a bunch of you are going to have an impromptu poetry slam or something on the East Bay 5:45. I always have to check to make sure that you're not secretly Zach Braff wearing a fake mustache or dressed as an old woman. Also, how do you all manage to smell like urine and some-how also Fritos? I am mystified.

Swearing off Fritos forever,

Liz

Dear iPod Guy,

I keep thinking I know you. Maybe not, but it just makes me wonder if you're the kind of boy who gets lost in the bookstores in the Mission or if you get dizzy when you smell eucalyptus trees too.

Sincerely,

Silly girl on the train

Dear Messrs. Anderson Cooper, Guy on the Verizon Commercial, and Henry Rollins,

In the past few weeks, several people have noted your sexual orientation when I've mentioned that I thought you were hot. This is just to let you know that I am fine with that and you're still my Silver Fox Boyfriend, my Can-Do Boyfriend, and my Scary Punk Tat-tooed Yet Sensitive Spoken Word Boyfriend, respectively.

Kisses on your naughty bits,

Liz

Dear Liz,

Just when you think you have a boring life and this city is wrong for you, you'll see a man walking down the sidewalk wearing ass-less chaps and a cape, and no one will even blink.

Remember that.

Love love love,

Liz

PS And also, you look very nice in the long skirt and pointy Manolos. Damn!

Dear Mattel,

So how's that whole "Screwing Up the Self-Image of Young Girls and Confused Boys with Freakishly Proportioned Fashion Dolls" thing working out for you? Great. Listen, you should really think about giving Ken a unit. Age 13 is NOT the time to find out that boys don't sport a small hard plastic nub. I'm just saying.

Thanks,

Liz

Dear iPod Guy,

Okay, I've decided that you and I knew each other in a past life. Maybe we just keep repeating over and over because we can't get it right. Maybe this is one of those times right now. Maybe I should talk to you. Maybe I should ask you what you're listening to on your iPod. Maybe I should go out and buy an iPod so that you'll have your white ear things in and I'll have my white ear things in and we'll look across the aisle at each other and smile. Maybe I should stop being silly.

Sincerely,

Liz

Dear Weekend,

I want to get naked with you right now. I mean it. I want you so bad. I want to lie in bed with you, in my flowered boxer shorts, and ignore all of the stuff I need to do around the apartment. I want to paint my toenails with you. I never want to let you go.

Sincerely,

Liz

Dear Aspartame,

Okay, are you *really* bad for me? I keep getting emails saying you'll give me MS or cancer, but then I also hear that it's total crap. So, tell me, are you going to kill me or what? Consider your answer carefully while I drink this Diet Coke.

Thirstily,
Liz

Dear Argyle Sock,

I was experimenting. I was kind of freaked out by the last laundromat I went to, which was apparently in the Tenderloin, where I am pretty sure that a hooker was turning tricks in the bathroom. So, I tried a new laundromat, one closer to the Mission. But really, all laundromats are the same, right? The smell of chlorine is still there, the weird fuzziness of the corners from tons of accumulated lint. The *spew* sound of the washers finishing their cycle. There was even the requisite college girl doing the wash in her pajama pants. And I was okay with the fact that I was the only English-speaking person in the place who was also wearing a bra. But I lost track of which dryer was mine and threw two socks into someone else's dryer. I tried to tell him that he had my socks, but he didn't speak English and the only Spanish word that comes to my brain for "sock" is profiláctico. Thus, I lost two socks, including you. Come back, pinky argyle with the green line through the diamonds. Please come back home. Lefty and I are waiting.

Leaving a light on for you,
Liz

Dear Ofelia Higgins,

Much to our shared dismay, I do not in fact have a penis and therefore cannot take advantage of your emailed offer to enlarge it. However, should the need ever, er, arise, I will certainly let you know.

Ksielja,
Liz

Dear iPod Guy,

Once upon a time, we were ancient. We were Vikings, set out to explore a new land. You were Gunther and I was Torvald and we had a love unrealized by other Vikings. We had to keep it a secret because we were at sea in a very small boat and tempers flared at the drop of a hat. You know, one of those helmets with horns coming out of them? Yeah, those. Don't drop one, it could put a hole in the boat. But it was a fine life. We'd steam up the sauna with our own heat and then retire between skins and feed each other gravlax and lefse. And then one day, you got into a fight with the minstrel and even though you were favored with 3-to-1 odds—due to your size and sexy flaring nostrils—the minstrel somehow skewered you with a pickle fork and went on to be called Ewald the Fighting Minstrel, while I was left alone to put lingonberry flowers on your pyre and swear that we would be together in Valhalla. And then I knocked Ewald on the head with a big rock and ran off into the fjords and froze to death.

Sincerely,
Liz

Dear Left Bra Strap,

Please stop slipping off my shoulder.

Sincerely,

Liz

Dear Guy with Green Bay Packer Vanity License Plate on His Hummer,

I realize that "PACKER" was probably already taken when you went to the DMV and maybe you panicked, never once imagining that someone else in California would have already claimed it for their own, and you were standing there at the counter with the million mouth breathers waiting in line behind you and the pressure was on. I understand. But "PCKER"? Think next time.

Sincerely,

Liz

Dear iPod Guy,

Once we were children at a Montessori. You were a paste eater and I had just had an accident and was walking around wearing a pair of borrowed sweatpants. You asked me if I wanted to help you build a fort with the big cardboard bricks, and I said okay. So we did. Later I watched in fascination as you used the leftie scissors. Then I pinched you and you called me a wiener and we never talked again and I grew up and you grew up somewhere else and you started a company that made parts of industrial machines and I got married to an accountant and volunteered at a library and learned the Dewey decimal system.

Sincerely,

Liz

Dear Bartender at the Irish Bank Pub,

I have seventeen twenty-dollar bills folded neatly in my bra because I don't want to carry a purse, so why won't you let me start a tab so that I can pay you later, after I've had a chance to visit the unisex bathroom and dig the wad out from under my boob pit? You know my assy friends forgot to stop at the ATM.

Sincerely,

Liz

Dear God,

Is that iPod Guy from the BART? He's not wearing his glasses and he doesn't have his iPod! How can I be sure? Give me a sign, God!

Thank you for these thine gifts
that we are about to receive,
Amen,
Liz

Dear God,

He left. With a girl. So much for mysterious ways.

Jesus wept,
Liz

Dear iPod Guy,

Once you were a double secret agent and I worked for the Kremlin and wore dark glasses and it was the fifties and I had a dark mole that hair grew out of because there were no Tweezermans in all of Mother Russia, but it was a sexy mole nonetheless. You liked it. Or at least one of your double secret agent personas did. And then I found out that you were a double secret agent and I was supposed to kill you and the broad shoulders of the KGB were coming, but I couldn't. We ran, hand in hand, and caught a train that snaked through the winter landscape until we reached Poland and then laughed in a bar and drank vodka until we got alcohol poisoning and died.

Sincerely,

Liz

Dear Guinness Dark Something Blargety Blarg,

Man, are you gross! And why won't my mouth stop watering?

Sincerely,

Liz

Der Bar,

You are the best bar EVER! And also, a very bad bar too! Very bad! And good! Woo!

BAd !

LIZ!

PP Shots are bad. Don't do shots. LIZ! DON'T DO SHOTS LIZ! Remember that.

Dear Chirpy Birds Living in the Trees Across the Street,

Shut. The. Fuck. Up.

Thank you.

Liz

PS This goes double for you, Nocturnal Chirpy Bird.

Dear Liz's Head,

Stupid.

Sincerely,

Everything below Liz's neck

Dear iPod Guy,

Where were you today? It's Monday?

Sincerely,

Liz

PS Maybe that wasn't you at the Irish Bank pub? Because I just don't think she's your kind of girl, with the big fake boobs and venture capitalist manicure.

Dear iPod Guy,

Actually, forget I said that. I can't go on like this anymore. I don't care if that was you with Hooker Hands. You're right. We should see other people.

Best regards,

Liz

Dear Fate,

Great. I can see *A Prayer for Owen Meany* sticking out of iPod Guy's messenger bag. Clearly this means that we are soul mates. Are we on the same page here, Fate? Are you with me? Fate? Is this thing on?

Sincerely,

Liz

PS Did I read that book on the train or not? I can't remember! Did he notice? Argh!

Dear iPod Guy,

Once we were living on the plains in a sod house and you wore broadcloth shirts that I sewed with big long loops of thread and I wore a petticoat made from a flour sack. You slaughtered a pig and we had to think up ways to use every single bit and you blew up the

bladder and tied a knot in it and then we played volleyball: me trip-
ping on my skirts and you with your shirt off, suspenders rubbing
your nipples raw, until the cow broke loose of her tethers and you
had to chase after her. Through a nest of rattlesnakes.

Sincerely,

Liz

Dear Stupid Job,

Downsizing who what now?

Sincerely,

Liz

PS I'm totally taking my stapler when I leave.

Dear Fucking Job,

Okay, it's been two hours and I'm not taking it personally anymore, as the emails have been flying all day and apparently the
magic number is ninety-one. I've been sitting in Union Square since
the riffing, watching tourists and reading emails on my MacBook
Pro, which apparently, I get to keep as a parting gift. I am glad that I
moved across the country to pay a thousand dollars a month to live
with a skeevy roommate who bogarts all my Trader Joe's stuff to get
the axe with two months of severance pay. Yeah.

Living the dream,

Liz

Dear iPod Guy,

I got on the train to go home, I looked around to see if you
were there. And for the first time since I got fired, for just one
brief moment, things didn't suck and I stopped feeling like someone had stamped a big cartoonish VOID across my forehead. But

you weren't there. I think I took an earlier train than normal, since I wasn't catching it from Embarcadero but rather from Union Station, so it threw off my timing completely. So, it's my own fault. And I'll never know. Maybe you would have said something. Maybe you would have smiled at me and I wouldn't have burst into tears, I would have smiled back and said hi and you would have said hi and then maybe you would have asked if I wanted to get coffee with you and you would have gotten off at my stop and we would have had tea and talked about goofy movies we've seen and how we both hate country music and then maybe we would have gone out for crepes or burritos or an independent movie or driven up to Napa and laughed at all the dot com millionaires and lived happily-ever-after-the-end.

Maybe.

Sincerely,

Liz

Dear iPod Guy,

Once we lived in the Paleolithic Era. I was a tribal leader and I clubbed you over the head because the way your ass looked in a deerskin made me grunt and jump up and down and I couldn't think until I got some of that. You were a woman and didn't like getting clubbed in the head and didn't talk to me until after you were nursing our infant and had another on the way. You set up a complicated water delivery system so that we didn't have to go out of the cave. I couldn't understand it, but it was beautiful. Truly beautiful. And then I got crushed by a woolly mammoth.

Sincerely,

Liz

Dear Liz,

I thought we agreed that doing shots at the Irish Bank was a bad idea.

Retchingly,

Liz

Dear Chirpy Birds,

I think I can buy a gun, but I don't think I can aim it well enough to hit you and not the hippies that live across the street. Curse you, Chirpy Birds. Curse you!

Oh, So Sincerely,

Liz

Dear Shaggy and Scooby,

Why the hell do you two always team up together and let Fred take Daphne and Velma? How is splitting Guy with Two Girls, leaving Guy with Dog a fair shake? Or is Fred actually being sexist in considering two women as much help as Scooby? Also, maybe you should not go scouting for snacks in those old run-down houses. Not only do you often run into scary monsters and the like, but that food can't be too fresh. Maybe go for a salad next time.

Sincerely,

Liz

Dear iPod Guy,

Do you notice that I'm not on the train anymore? Just wondering.

Sincerely,

Liz

Dear Starbucks,

So, the plan is to get up every morning, get dressed like normal, jump on the BART, and go into the city to get a job. The plan is *not* to stop at one of your eighty bazillion locations and spend more of my quickly dwindling severance check. So, yeah, that's the plan. So tomorrow when I come in and order my standard venti nonfat, no whip mocha, could you be a sweetie and just say "Um, no"? I'm glad that we are both in agreement.

Weak but adorable,

Liz

PS You're putting crack in the coffee, right? That's why it costs so much?

Dear Crack,

Is there something better than you? I have no interest in crack myself, but people look at me funny when I say the new TV show is the Kate Spade of television, or a pastry is the Manolo Blahnik of eclairs or that dirty himbo is the BMW of singer/songwriters.

Sincerely,

Liz

Dear iPod Guy,

Smile. Eyebrow raise. Prolonged eye contact. Tummy flutter. Hello, you.

Sincerely,

Liz

Dear iPod Guy,

Once we were trees in California, giant redwoods. Your leaves would whirl around my roots and I would creak and bat my limbs at you. We stood through centuries, always eighty yards apart, never able to intermingle our branches. I would blush each year that I lost my foliage and you would growl in a way that only trees can growl. And then we were gone. Stupid root rot.

Sincerely,

Liz

Dear Sarah Jessica Parker,

You might think that I am still having residual bitterness over the fact that you married my boyfriend, Ferris Bueller, but I still must tell you that I think you look like a praying mantis.

Sincerely,

Liz

Dear iPod Guy,

Once I was Judy Garland and you were Clark Gable and it was 1939 and I was working on a little picture called *The Wizard of Oz* and you were one set over, doing that big Civil War picture, and we hid in the back lots and exchanged torrid glances at each other until Jimmy Stewart yelled at us. You asked me to kiss you and I did and your mustache smelled like cigars and I told you about Munchkins looking up my skirt and making jokes about how ruby slippers reflect up. But then you misunderstood my thing with Mickey Rooney and were hurt. So we kept on making movies and got married to other people and made babies and money, until Marilyn Monroe and the Beatles ruined everything. I saw you again once in Vegas. I was doing a show at the Aladdin, but by then you were an alcoholic and I was pretty much just stringing from one pill to the next, but we both looked at each other and smiled, and if there was a God in heaven, Mickey Rooney had one of his heart attacks right then.

Sincerely,

Liz

Dear Gainful Employment,

Remember me? Hello? Anyone? Bueller?

Sincerely,

Liz

Dear Skeevy Roommate,

I'm putting an ad on Craigslist.com to find someone to sublet my room. Hope you get someone cool and who will let you smoke pot in the apartment. Sorry. I'll email you my forwarding address when I get back home, but until then, here's my parents' address and their phone number. In case anyone stops by for me or anything. Not like they will, but, you know, just in case.

Sincerely,

Liz

Dear iPod Guy,

Once we were sitting on a train in San Francisco. You have little white earphones in your ears and your head bowed down, watching the beat of your fingers drumming against your leg. Your Paul Frank messenger bag is tucked behind your feet and you need a haircut and I wonder if you aren't one of those Dot Commers that work in an industrial loft and take motorized scooters to meetings in SoMa. I am alone, a glorified office drone from the Embarcadero, posing like some Mary Tyler Moore fantasy in Banana Republic and knock-off Marc Jacobs. I watch everything, too busy thinking up silly things to entertain myself so that I won't have time to think anything else, watching the sun dapple in staccato rhythm against the seats with the rails murmuring beneath our feet, and it is one of those rare moments when everything is exactly where it is supposed to be: me, you, everything. There is a brief, breathtaking glimpse of the Pacific and a golden glow turns the famed hills into a perfect Disney backdrop, and you, the one person who seems real through all of this, are sitting right there across the aisle from me, and I think, for a moment, that maybe anything is possible. Anything. Then the doors open.

Sincerely,

Liz

FEÐGIN

THE DARKNESS MAKES EVERYTHING RISKY, EVERY STEP FRAUGHT WITH IN-
visible scuttling, chittering of tiny creatures—mice, perhaps, terres-
trial birds imagined—or invisible elves—under step. We are near
Bárðarbunga, Iceland, a recently quiet volcano, and in the distance,
a house that was once a house. Half of the house is now covered
with a lava flow, cooled rock spills out of the windows, and the other half emerges from that rock, crushed slightly, as though exhausted by the weight of everything, as though it were sighing, being
either consumed by or born from the fire.

My father is a genius. One of the evil kinds. He intends to end
the world. "The safest place for us," he says, "is here, almost on top
of the world."

We had to come here, where no one knows us. He didn't mean
to cause an explosion. People turning colors. Pieces of asteroids
falling through whole, refraining from their usual burn in the atmo-
sphere. It was a setback.

I don't want people to get hurt. I don't want to run somewhere else. Where would we even go? So I tinker with his concoctions whenever he isn't looking, whenever he goes on his "thinking walks" in the lava fields. "Don't step on the moss, Poppa!" I say, but what I'm really saying is "Stay out there longer, I need to save us. I need to save us all." Then I tuck my fingers into the tiny gears and wiggle them loose, erase schematics, break wires, and drip honey onto cooling units. Now his inventions never work right. His bombs fizzle. His death lasers fail to even burn paper, much less explode the moon.

My father isn't really evil, he just thinks big. I believe he knows that I mess with his work. I suspect he lingers on his walks, talking to the elves, pleading with the aurora for the next big idea that will take out the villains in power.

"Who do they think they are, Maeve?" he says to me in the mornings, which don't feel like mornings because of the night sky, only skyr and cloudberry jam to mark the new day. "How can they let the police run the government? They are insane! Inmates are running the asylum. The president wraps himself up in a flag while bending over the constitution and dropping a steaming turd right on it." He can never keep from reading the American papers.

"We're in Iceland now, Poppa," I say, pulling gently at the paper. "This is our home now. Why does it matter what they do?" It matters greatly to him. The new president is, I fear, one of the people Poppa wants most to touch with the death laser.

I replace my father's newspapers with novels, try to redirect his passions, but they become just another steam vent to fuel his grandiosity and desire for retribution: He will always see himself as the hero. He draws on the tablecloth. This time it clearly involves a giant drill into the earth. I roll my eyes.

Sometimes while he works, I take walks by myself. I visit the house with the cooled lava rock. If the house weren't here, I wouldn't know this lava was special. If the lava weren't here, the house wouldn't be special. Did the people know it was coming? Did they get out and leave in time? It must have felt like the world was on fire. Now, the air is cold and pure.

Back home, Poppa draws on napkins, tea towels, the bare white walls. At night, when he falls asleep into his fish chowder by the fireplace, I open his latest creations and manipulate them. Pick connections apart, untwist spark plugs from their moorings, redirect reflection mirrors.

Together, we push and pull toward and away from each other, house and rock, tide and the shore.

THE BOG KING

I DROVE MY RENTAL CAR STRAIGHT FROM THE DUBLIN AIRPORT TO THE
museum, but I still managed to miss the staff, who had all left for
the night. I was greeted by the museum guard—tired, eyeing up
a Thermos against the cold dark. I knew without knowing that it
probably contained more than coffee, so I affected my best—or
worst—Appalachian accent, appealing to his blue-collar roots, or
whatever they call it in the Emerald Isle. Maybe the working class
wore green? I was wearing my great-grandmother's favorite brooch,
a glittering owl with two large diamond eyes and citrine feathers,
grasping a green chalcedony branch. I took care to cover it with an
obviously hand-knit scarf. If he had seen the jewels, he certainly
would have balked and shut me out, he was the type. Hell, I was
the type too. I shouldn't have even worn it to travel in, it was too
dear, but I had brief hopes of getting an upgrade on the transatlan-
tic flight. Sometimes that worked. It hadn't worked this time, but it

was definitely a good luck charm hidden under my layers because he shrugged and decided I was boring enough to be a research scientist. I promised him I just wanted to be calm, stay out of his way, really, I wanted to set up my workstation and apply the first coat to the specimen, that's all, but he was already going back to his desk and small television.

I often joked that I was descended from lumber barons, railroad barons, but really, my grand-barons hadn't pillaged land. They had pillaged people, had run factories where retirement funds weren't necessary because the workers rarely retired, either choosing to die stooped over their workstations or picking up the rare forms of malignancy that for some reason weren't very rare in the buildings that bore my mother's family name. My ancestors wouldn't have approved of my line of work or, really, my line of "very erudite volunteerism," as the trust attorney liked to call it. When I made preparations for this trip, he had savored that line once again, rolling it around in his mouth like a pearl onion, and I had to suffer through it until he handed off my money. *My* money.

I liked to say that my family had left me orphaned but comfortable. I had some trust money that kept me from being homeless, but just barely. Tenure jobs in my field are less common than unicorns, and you practically had to wait for someone to die to get their job, but I never thought I'd be pushing forty and still doomed to an adjunct's life of making less than $2K per month without medical benefits.

My coterie of past roommates always picked on my penchant for wearing my brooch. One thing I learned from my family, stingy, withholding relatives that they were, is that real wealth always recognizes their own kind. That stupid owl brooch had gotten me into just enough places and rubbing elbows with just enough of the right kind of people. I always felt moments away from getting the big patron to support what my great-aunt liked to refer to as my "unfortunate history habit."

Once inside the antiquity's lab, I found that nothing had been prepared for my work, but this was to be expected—everything is underfunded and academics are generally more interested in their own research unless they could get a co-credit. But there it was, my date for the night and I had it all to myself.

When the workers had found Cloonageeher Man, the body was curled in a fetal position. One femur had been snapped in two by the peat threshing machine, but there were also signs of ritualistic overkilling. They thought the body was a recent murder victim. *Recent*, they had thought, as in the last few years, maybe a decade at most. Its thoughtful eyes closed to the damp morning, its hair dyed red by the tannins in the sphagnum. A fresh kill.

Most bog bodies look like deflated people-shaped balloons at best, unidentifiable misshapen clumps of trash marked by small, terrible reminders of humanity: a blob with a perfect foot, a flattened football that turns out to be a crushed head, or like Kayhausen Boy, looking very much like a discarded and dirty snowsuit that some child had forgotten after a busy day of make-believe.

But Cloonageeher Man was mostly there, recognizable, unmistakably male, impressively rendered in its humanity, complete with a hammered copper armband. There was also a grinning slice under its chin, followed by a braided leather cord that may have hung the body after death or completed the dirty execution that had been botched in a rush or in a passion.

"Hello, handsome," I said. Maybe that was what did it, some kind of incantation. Handsome it was not, but I had started mentally referring to it as Clooney just the same. The face was one of the better bog faces I had seen with only slight compression and eyelashes still intact and resting on the gritty brow as though it were still sleeping. The skin was rumpled and dark bronze, looking like an expensive leather throw one might buy in a fancy mall. Its chin still had stubble; its mouth was closed, holding back murdered secrets.

I had a powerful urge to lean over and kiss the lips but caught myself. The things we think when we are all alone. Ultimately, people in charge of seductive human remains had done far worse. Eva Peron's embalmed body, for instance, and that doctor in Key West who fell in love with his terminal tuberculosis patient. What was a little kiss?

The team had done the medical imaging already, so we already knew the body still had internal organs. That itself wasn't unusual. Usually bog bodies were murdered in a seemingly rushed affair, without the formal preparations for burial; however, this one also had bones, which was very rare with bog bodies, especially ones as old as Cloonageeher Man. The bog juices and plant matter keep the soft tissues and even the fingernails looking pristine. The half-moons along the fingernail beds looked as though Clooney was only a nightmare away from startling awake, but the sphagnum generally leached out calcium, one thing healthy bones need. There must have been something special about the flora of that particular bog where it had rested millennia, something about its long nap that made this one special.

Sphagnum moss was capable of holding over twenty-five times as much water as itself. Sometimes, I felt like sphagnum moss: overly full of history and worries and inappropriate impulses. But unlike my anxiety, sphagnum prevented human remains from putrefying, essentially leaving the body preserved but sometimes crushed, eventually, by the weight of water and time. *Some kind of Iron Age magic tea*, I had written in my grant proposal for this project, which was denied.

Cloonageeher Man was so freshly pulled from that quiet internment, a midpoint between earth and water that lacked oxygen, that its preserved flesh was still pure. Exposure to the air was only just starting to oxidize the muscle. Left out of the bog environment, the body hardens and loses plasticity, recoils as time itself speeds up or perhaps unravels, first cracking and then flaking, turning powdery and eventually crumbling into dust in the period of just a few months.

To combat this rapid deterioration, I had tapped criminal forensic scientists who had been experimenting with a way to revive desiccated skin to help with body identification, retrieving fingerprints and identifying scars on corpses long exposed to more brutal elements. It was worth a shot the next time they pulled up a juicy one, and given the decades before bog body discovery, I never thought I'd get a chance only a year after my paper was published theorizing this treatment. And then, the invitation from the museum and a quick money tap from my dwindling resources and here I was and here it was, Clooney, my golden boy who would deliver me tenure on a silver platter.

The chemical broth, trademarked "Bryo-Vital," smelled of moss— Icelandic this time and full of antioxidants. These days, Bryo-Vital was frequently used in forensic science for skin preservation as a much better alternative to urea or sodium carbonate solution, but first, it was an essential part of the beauty regimen for rich wives. Those women anointed their décolletage with the mossy liquor, noting that it really did reverse sun damage from their bikini-wearing vacations in Bimini, Palm Springs, Monaco, or wherever else the nouveau riche went these days. I still identified with old money enough to disdain the newly wealthy, even though I never had any actual money myself. I was what those with money called a "poor relation." It was my lot in life to be invited to distant family weddings and arrive with empty Tupperware in my tote bag so that I could dine on leftover prime rib. It would be better after tenure though. It would be better after I documented and preserved Clooney and took my place among the paleoanthropology glitterati.

I started with the face, using a cosmetic-grade fan brush I purchased at a Sephora that smelled like lilies and copper, balanced with acrid indulgence and need. I had to put it on my credit card but kept the receipts in case the university thought I'd had a cosmetics splurge on their dime. The Bryo-Vital goop was cool to the touch. I applied a very light skim of it over Clooney's amber skin. Up close, all of the pores, tendons, veins on a particularly strong-looking forearm were visible. Was that a very delicate scar? Perhaps chicken pox? The first coat of gel quenches oxidation. The next evening, I planned to sink the body into a tank full of the stuff, some seven thousand dollars' worth of fancy Beverly Hills housewife goo.

Already the facial skin I had treated looked more wholesome, a bit more vital. The reality of the body was hard to parse; Clooney had looked like a tattered doll when I had arrived, but now, with the glistening salve, its skin was plumped up, looking more like roasted meat, like pork or perhaps a leaner game cut, like venison.

I lost myself in the minutia, poring over its fundament with delicate kisses of the brush, *whisk whisk whisk.* The slurry turned bronze as well, the tannins oozing forward, a smell like burnt coffee and mushroom and sewage, but somehow savory, like rotting beef stew. Venison, I corrected myself, its hand in mine, fingers outstretched, the index finger tickling my wrist while I brushed the goop around its thumb.

I had made it all the way down to the inner thigh when I heard a sound. *Chaaaaaa wish*. It was an owlish sound, a keening.

Dia hish

Again. It was the sound of something papery shuffling against dry wood.

Dia hswith

I leaned back on the work stool and craned my neck to look through the open door down the hallway. The security guard was sure to be around. "Hello?" My voice echoed down the corridor. This was the beginning to every horror movie, the penultimate scene before a killer wearing a sporting mask stabs the heroine through the head with a machete. "Hello?"

Dia dwish. The sound again.

I leaned forward and looked at Clooney. Its eyelids un-shuttered, revealing empty places where eyeballs had once been. This too had occurred in its kinsman Grauballe Man. Clooney's eyeballs had shriveled and marbleized under the pressure of plant matter. There was nothing there, a dark clot of tissue in each socket, a mottled raisin that might once have been bright green or a dazzling hazel.

It was fascinating to see the body begin to articulate its extremities. The eyelid membranes were so thin; it wasn't surprising that they should move slightly as the moisturizing liquid rehydrated the cells. I snapped several pictures of Clooney's face, the lashes parted, the eyebrows seeming to furrow now.

Everyone who had inspected Clooney agreed that it was definitely an overkill specimen, likely a former king, given the body's location near a king-making hill. In Clooney's case, the leather garrote was still wrapped around its throat, which also had been sliced open, and the skull was crushed, which might have been the result of a bludgeoning, or done postmortem. Clooney was scheduled to be undressed, and the archaeologists firmly expected to find stab wounds under its wrappings. The unveiling would be delayed until the photographers from *National Geographic* were available, which could be a week or more.

I scrawled a reminder, *do more research into the Sleeping Beauty of Capuchin*, a child who died of pneumonia after World War I and was essentially mummified and is now displayed in the catacombs. With temperature fluctuations, her tiny eyelids open partially from time to time, revealing intact bright blue eyes, but of course, that body was only ninety years old and had been interred with a more modern chemical cocktail of zinc, glycerin, and aspirin. On second thought, I also wrote *Lady Dai Zhui?* and underlined it. Lady Dai Zhui might have walked the planet at the same time as Clooney, roughly 300 to 100 BC. Not only were her mummified organs intact and her limbs flexible, but the blood in her veins could even be ABO typed. To this day, researchers have not been able to figure out how she was prepared for mummification, or why.

There was something fascinating about how we treat and mistreat our dead. Women generally seemed to get the brunt of it, although here we were, roles reversed, Clooney on the table, and I with my fancy makeup brush. I thought again about the trust attorney suggesting I go into mortuary science instead of archeological. At least it would provide a living wage, but I would have to deal with fresh grief, identities, legacies, and mistreated relations cut out of endowments.

Diar wish. The feathery sound again, prickling the back of my neck. I dropped my fan brush to the floor. It sounded like the noise was right there next to me. The sound of a knife being sharpened on a leather strap.

Clooney's lips had previously been pressed together, but now they appeared to be parting, or opening; the jaw seemed to be un-clenching as the elixir did its work to saturate the ligaments and sinew.

I took another photo and flipped backward to check the previ-ous ones—the lips had definitely begun to get plumper and were closed before. Clooney's last moments had still been evident on its face, a grim expression of endurance that it had worn throughout millennia. Now it was changing. My actions were changing it. Bryo-Vital was more powerful than I had originally anticipated—less than an ounce applied to the mandibular area had penetrated the hinge joints, and gravity now pulled it forward out of the postmortem eternal clench. I wrote furiously on a fresh sheet in my notebook.

Jihar witchhhhh. A sense of movement out of the corner of my eye. His face, the eyes, his mouth. *Diaarrrr winch.* His lips were out of alignment, air sucking from somewhere inside his body, a hidden fissure or stab wound through the ribs, inflating his old compressed, preserved lungs.

What I wanted to say was "How is this happening," what I want-ed to do was run away and find the guard, what I wanted to think about was a job offer from Harvard and getting tenure, what I want-ed to do was kiss his mouth and wake up because I was clearly hav-ing a jet lag hallucination, and what I did instead was remain sitting on the stool and say "Oh, it's you."

The burnt corks in his eye sockets moved in concert toward the owl brooch pinned to my sweater lapel, glittering under the harsh examination lights.

His fingers flexed, twitching.

"Diar wish." It was old Gaelic. *Hello,* he was saying. *Hello again.* We might only have moments together. Minutes. Seconds. Harvard. Maybe I'd prefer the weather in Stanford more. The staff would be here in the morning. This moment would never come again.

I picked up the fan brush and dipped it into the forensic balm. "Hello, handsome." I said again. How this must seem to him, to be one moment a king and the next, lying on a steel autopsy table. How I must seem to him.

I brushed the saliva-like goop around his parched lips while picking up my phone to film. In frame, out of focus, the brush working around his mouth while the autofocus worked to settle on his brittle leather fingers, reaching out toward the camera.

ACKNOWLEDGMENTS

Stories in this collection were previously published, some in different forms, at the following:

"Strange Magic" (as **"Skate Queen"**) was published in *ANMLY* #25. Nominated for Pushcart Prize, 2018.

"Ghosting" was published in *NonBinary Review* #10.

"Where She Went" was originally published in *Per Contra* #27 and reprinted in *Spillwords*, June 2019.

"Lower Midnight" was published in *Paper Darts*, July 2012.

"INGOB" was published in *Barrelhouse* #14.

"Passeridae" was originally published in *Blackbird*, Fall 2010. Nominated for Best New Voices, 2008; nominated for Pushcart Prize, 2010. Reprinted in *Fresh.Ink*, Summer 2020.

"Texts From Beyond" was published in *Jet Fuel Review*, Spring 2019.

"Seven Minutes in Heaven" (as **"Osculation"**) was published in *Waxwing*, May 2019.

"Intersomnolence" was published in *Drunken Boat* #12.

"Billet-Doux" was originally published in *Barrelhouse* #3 and *The Evansville Review*, July 2018.

"Feðgin" was published in *Syntax and Salt*, October 2017.

"The Bog King" was published in *Jet Fuel Review*, Fall 2020.

THANK YOUS

I'm grateful for the support of the editors of the journals and magazines who published these stories initially, particularly Dave Housley and Joe Killian, who picked up "Billet-Doux" back in the early days of *Barrelhouse* and invited me to read it at the KGB Bar in New York so many years ago. Little did we all know what a monster they unleashed. They continue to be treasures of the literary community and I feel very honored that they let me hang out with them at conferences.

I've been incredibly fortunate to work with many great authors who offered advice and clean reads while I developed these stories. It's impossible to name all of them, but I know for a fact that without Liam Callanan, George Makana Clark, Jincy Willett, Jean Thompson, Lynda Barry, Dan Chaon, Maile Chapman, Gwynne Kennedy, and Doug Unger these stories would still be floundering in my draft folder. I'm also grateful to the supportive writing spaces at the University of Nevada at Las Vegas, the Black Mountain Institute, and the University of Wisconsin-Milwaukee, all of which have given these words a stage, an audience, and a home.

I was so lucky to work with Christine Stroud from Autumn House Press. A great editor is such an incredible collaboration, and the process was very warm and nurturing that I was kind of sad when we finished. I'm indebted to her and the amazing Deesha Philyaw, the judge of the AHP Fiction Prize, for their belief in this collection.

Other people who have contributed greatly to these stories include my perennial readers Jake Kenny, Michael Moore, Monique van den Berg, Jen Larsen, Kate Harding, Lindsay Rhean Griffin, Illanit Moskul, Tonya Todd, Christina Clancy, Amanda Skenandore, Oksana Marafioti, Alex Galt, Amy Mazzariello, Melissa Gorzelancyzk, Molly Ann Magestro, and above all, my sister Amy Fleming, who was my very first audience and patron of my funny/scary/sad sense of stories. I'm very fortunate to have fantastic and supportive writing groups, including S.L. Winton, M. A. Hurley, Chelsi Hicks, Mary Kate DeJardin, Eric Duran-Valle, Eileen Snider, Meghan Bonikowski, Adria Cruz Tabor, Sam Goodman, Alexandra Murphy, Dayneé Alejandra Rosales, Flavia Stefani, Dylan Fisher, Robert Ren, Cody Gambino, Jordan Sutlive, Sara Tausenfreund, Sam Smith, Joe Milan Jr, Oscar Oswald, Carrieann Cahall, and Wendy McClure.

These stories are in many ways love letters to my own favorite authors, whose impressions and fingerprints are all over these plots, characters, and phrases. As well as so many already mentioned above, this collection was very much influenced by the works of Kazuo Ishiguro, Robert Olen Butler, Lesley Marmon Silko, Carmen Maria Machado, Margaret Atwood, Mary Godwin Shelley, Lorrie Moore, Elizabeth McCracken, John Irving, Douglas Coupland, Jane Austen, Amanda Davis, T.C. Boyle, Raymond Carver, Louise Erdrich, Joyce Carol Oates, Shirley Jackson, and Joy Harjo. I hope these authors will forgive my paying homage to them the best way I knew how, in tiny coded shoutouts and embedded references.

I am very fortunate to have a devoted Gentleman Caller in Steven J. Schuchart Jr., who frequently reminds me that there is writing to be done and makes space in our lives for me to practice, hone, and dither over sentences. He is the very best personal champion and it's impossible to overstate how much this collection would not exist if not for him.

And thank you, gentle reader, for being there. We're in this together.

NEW AND FORTHCOMING

Seed Celestial by Sara R. Burnett
WINNER OF THE 2021 AUTUMN HOUSE POETRY PRIZE
SELECTED BY EILEEN MYLES

Bittering the Wound by Jacqui Germain
WINNER OF THE 2021 CAAPP BOOK PRIZE
SELECTED BY DOUGLAS KEARNEY

The Running Body by Emily Pifer
WINNER OF THE 2021 AUTUMN HOUSE NONFICTION PRIZE
SELECTED BY STEVE ALMOND

The Scorpion's Question Mark by J. D. Debris
WINNER OF THE 2022 DONALD JUSTICE POETRY PRIZE
SELECTED BY CORNELIUS EADY

Given by Liza Katz Duncan
WINNER OF THE 2022 RISING WRITER PRIZE IN POETRY
SELECTED BY DONIKA KELLY

Ishmael Mask by Charles Kell

Origami Dogs: Stories by Noley Reid